MW00790324

This is a work of fiction. N
incidents either are the product of the author's imagination or
are used fictitiously. Any resemblance to actual persons, living
or dead, events, or locales is entirely coincidental.

Cover art by Miblart.

First Paperback Edition
ISBN: 978-1-7349634-3-4

In memory of Carmen and my grandparents.

OUTLAW

A MASON JONES THRILLER: BOOK 2

ANTHONY DECAPITE

CHAPTER ONE

've been a thief. I've been an imposter. I was almost a killer.

I was on a new path, but the cold voice was still there. It sent a chill up my spine and told me I'd never be more than a lost ex-con spending the rest of my days in limbo, never able to right my wrongs. The voice was loudest at night.

It was quieter now, with Josh Ortiz next to me and the view of Franklin Canyon Reservoir stretching out in front of us. I'd been out for eight months, and for Ortiz it'd been over a year.

The reservoir wasn't picture-perfect. The water was low, pink confetti tittered on the cattails—a gender reveal party?—and doggie poop bags lurked under the bushes. Why bring bags, pick up the turd, and tie it up only to leave it? Didn't make sense. The blue dome of the sky was tainted with smog on the horizon, and to the east, a chalky haze fanned out, compliments of the Bakersfield-area

Prince Fire. Only a 5% chance of rain, but that was a good thing. It meant it'd be harder to contain, and that meant the wildland firefighter crews would need me. I'd have a chance to right my wrongs. Not perfect…but hummingbirds trilled, turtles bobbed in the water, and the afternoon sun wicked away the traces of sweat on my scalp.

My short, stocky, tattoo-covered friend picked a fallen cattail off the ground. There was a 100% chance of him making a dirty joke about the penis-shaped plant.

"How much room you got in your pack?" he asked. "New side hustle: disposable dildos."

I smirked. I was the Dallas Raines of predicting Ortiz.

"Natural…biodegradable…girthy," I said. "It's a good angle."

Ortiz held up one covered in pond scum and made a face.

"Your mom's been here."

"You sure it wasn't Rayna?" I asked. I could personally vouch for his cousin having a high libido—she'd "rehabilitated" me several times the week I got out of prison—but she never wanted to cuddle and she'd moved on quicker than fire burns uphill. To a guy named *Chet.* I was still salty about it.

"*Pito*," Ortiz said.

I decided not to mention the spicy things Rayna'd said about *my* pito and opened my pack, pulling out a bottle in a cooling wrap.

"I figured shot glasses would break."

He grinned at the tequila. Bumping along the road of life, you get a mishmash of passengers hopping on and off the bus. I was damn lucky Josh Ortiz ended up on mine, even though I barely got to see the stumpy asshole anymore—and I lived in his back yard.

What can you do? The wheels on the bus go round and round…

"Did I do good?" I asked. His favorite was supposedly *reposado*, but I'd noticed him bringing *anejo* home a lot these days. My tongue couldn't tell the difference.

"It's perfect," he said.

A knot in my stomach relaxed. The voice was barely a whisper now. We were free and we had an afternoon to drink some (apparently) good tequila. I popped open the tequila *extra anejo* for the first toast.

Ortiz had been in the game since he was thirteen, and in the Sureños since fourteen. We'd gotten help from the gang for a murder mission targeting Grayson Graham, but when I decided not to kill him, Ortiz and I had taken on a debt. The way the Sureños made us pay it off was by transporting $10 million in cash from Reno to Tijuana. Just some casual interstate-to-international trafficking of laundered money for an organized crime gang, risking federal prison and rival gang hits—while on parole. Inhaling the oaky, vanilla scent wafting from the *anejo,* I thought: *Thank God the trip was so boring.* That job had settled our debt *and* gotten him out of the Sureños. That, along with a promise of lifelong silence, finally made us free.

"We did it," I said, swigging and passing it to him.

"Hell yeah, we did," he said.

It was a lot mellower than I expected, but still had a tangy quality. I was more of a whiskey and beer kinda guy, but damn if it didn't feel good. I wanted to shout out victory to the world. Hell, why not?

I crowed to the water, earning me a *quack-quack* clapback

from a pair of ducks. Ortiz yipped out a damn fine imitation of a coyote, sending them flapping into the air. The burn of the tequila spread outward from my chest, and we toasted and drank to the future. We toasted to my EMT certification and we toasted to his animal shelter job. We toasted to each other, "Brothers from another mother!" We toasted to the living—Ortiz's girls—and we toasted to the dead—my brother Caleb and the OGs Ortiz had lost along the way. We toasted to something I didn't understand because Ortiz said half of it in Spanish, laughing while he did.

"I turn thirty this year," I groaned.

"You old fuck. And Emily is turning five. Starts kindergarten in the fall…"

"Going too fast," I said.

"Trust," Ortiz agreed.

The family man. He was five years younger and acted like a thirteen-year-old half the time, but somehow he'd always been more of an adult than me. I lived in a motorhome I didn't own, got around on an ancient Ducati, and was drowning in debt. Ortiz was so far ahead. A house (inherited from his *abuela,* but still). A steady, decent-paying job that he also happened to love. A baby momma and a kid. A *kid.*

I couldn't keep my eyes off the confetti and poop bags tainting the vegetation. They were mocking me.

"You're a baby, then you're a kid, then you're an adult. What a world," I said. A kid who doesn't know his ass from his elbow, and then suddenly…you're not? You're supposed to take on the world, ass-elbow confusion be damned? And then breeders like Ortiz had their own babies. It was mind-blowing. Or maybe it was the tequila.

The wheels on the bus go round and round… I chortled at myself.

"You crossed the border!"

From buzzed to drunk, he meant. Was I? He's said I'm a very philosophical drunk.

The plastic of one poop bag was transparent enough for me to see the condensation inside: drops trickling onto lumps. That was the last straw. I started picking up the trash and shoving it into my pack.

"Bucket Man over here," Ortiz said.

I smiled at that. He'd been the Bucket Man at the LAC prison health care facility when we'd met. He'd been running a grift and, when I noticed, pulled a blade on me. Now he was my brother.

Ortiz joined me and we filled up the pack, passing the tequila back and forth until he waved it off.

"If we keep going, I'ma fall down the mountain. Trust," Ortiz said.

I capped the bottle, head rushing as I stood and shouldered the pack. The waterfront thicket was a bit greener on our way out. We took a side loop to extend the hike and walk off the booze. We got lost for a while and hiked a lot more than we meant to.

When we stumbled to the car, dusty and warm, we'd come down to a mellow buzz. Still, we checked our levels on his Bluetooth BAC test. The last thing two ex-cons needed was a DUI. The breathalyzer said we were both safe to drive, and I was surprised to find my levels lower than his.

I took the keys and breathed in the dappled sunlight stretching over the gravel lot and nearby houses. The haze of the Prince Fire caught that light and took on a dirty orange shade. Calling out to me. I was free. I was ready. *I'm coming.*

Despite the litter and haze, California was beautiful.

We piled in the car. I pointed at the clock, which showed a bit past 4 pm.

"Your parole officer going to be upset?" I asked.

"Not if I give her my gift," Ortiz chortled. "Some guys get whiskey dick. Tequila has the opposite effect for me."

"Keep it in your pants. I'm staying under the speed limit all the way back."

Ortiz rolled down the window, breathing in the mountain air. "Ohhhh, I can feel it. I'm definitely gonna put another baby in her."

I laughed and started back.

When we pulled up, Ortiz's family was in the front yard taking advantage of the nice weather. His "parole officer," Veronica Narvaez, smiled from the porch, and his daughter, Emily, yelled out, "Daddy, watch!" as she slid headfirst down a playset slide and then sprang back to her feet like she'd performed an amazing feat.

"Wow!" he exclaimed, and knelt down as his other little girl, Penny the pit mix, launched herself at him to lather his face with her tongue.

"My favorite girl!" Ortiz crooned, sweeping the charcoal-gray dog up in his arms, eyes twinkling at his daughter.

"Daddy!" Emily huffed.

Vee made a *you're hilarious* face and came over. He put Penny down and dipped Vee devilishly low for a lingering kiss. She stood back up, punch-drunk and smiling. Drawn-on eyebrows aside, his

Afro-Latina princess was adorable. They went well together. Their daughter mystified me. Emily stood waist-high and had all her dad's swagger.

Penny gave me a lick on the hand and I scratched her behind the ears.

"You do a good job keeping guard?" Ortiz liked the dog to watch over his ladies when he wasn't around.

Emily tapped me and pointed to a mostly empty plate with a few deformed dino-nuggies on it.

"Do you want some?"

"No, but thank you." I didn't know how to be around kids, but one thing I remembered from time-served was that I hated being *treated* like one. So instead of baby-talk, I tended to overcorrect.

"It's because they look like poop," she said sagely.

"You are your father's daughter, kid."

Ortiz crowded onto the playset slide, which went no higher than his knees, and Emily ran over to explain he was too big. Ortiz pretended not to understand. While they played, Vee caught my attention.

"Mace."

I went by Mason now. Mace was the name of a thief and a liar, but I didn't bother correcting her. Ortiz was grandfathered in, and by extension, so was his baby momma. Even though, judging by the bend of the make-up eyebrows, I was about to be nagged.

I forced a cheery smile on my face so Ortiz wouldn't think things amiss if he looked over. Vee and I had never gotten along. She was jealous: fine with him drinking buckets of tequila on their date nights, but hated him having fun with someone who wasn't her. And while she wouldn't come right out and say it, she thought I was a bad influence. I used to think it was because she didn't know what Ortiz and I had been through together. Now I think it was because she did.

"I can smell the tequila. Did you at least use the breathalyzer?" she asked.

"I'm not sure. We did a lot of crack, and some black tar heroin too. It's a little hazy."

"How's the apartment search?" She ignored my joke and moved onto her favorite topic.

"Just getting started. Been a bit busy lately," *freeing your man from the worst influence of his life, the Sureños.* I kept that one in the chamber, but she caught the bullet in her teeth anyway.

"That trip you took? Maybe don't be so proud of helping to clean up a mess *you* made."

My face heated. She wasn't wrong.

"He's the one that joined the Sureños, okay?" I reminded her, frustrated. "I'll get out of your hair as soon as I can."

"My nappy hair," she said with icy sweetness.

I winced. Emily had hugged me once and I'd noticed that her hair, while dark, was less tightly coiled. "Will it get nappier when she gets older?" I'd asked Vee after Emily scampered off.

"Excuse me?" Vee'd replied, gaping at me.

"Like, is nappy hair a dominant trait or does it blend with other hair traits?"

Vee had refused to talk to me for a week and I'd learned a valuable lesson: never use the word "nappy" to describe African-heritage hair. My stomach listed every time I remembered it. I hadn't known the word was taboo—I was raised in a trailer park, for fuck's sake. But still... I wasn't trying to "otherize" Emily or Vee. *That* word I learned when I was trying to understand what I'd done wrong.

"I'll leave you to it," I said, ready to get out of this, and she let me retreat. We were probably never going to be friends. I nodded to Ortiz, "Later, bro," and he shot me a grin as Vee ushered her family inside the house.

I opened the side gate and went around back, stooping to check on my six-herb planter set. I took a deep whiff, using it to cleanse my palate of that conversation. I lingered over my favorite: rosemary. The woody aroma brought my blood pressure down a notch or two. Some ex-cons find religion. I found gardening.

I tossed the trail trash in the garbage bin, giving my pack a good sniff check. All clear, no ruptures, *and* I'd done my good deed for the day. In the waning light, the stripes of the 1973 Starcraft Starcruiser looked gold instead of mustard yellow, which was nice. I went inside. The motorhome interior had even stronger 70s vibes than the exterior, with brown shag carpet, plaid orange cushions, and faux-woodgrain laminate surfaces. I opened the windows and turned on a box fan. The one-piece fiberglass body didn't soak up heat as much as other vehicles, but it was still warm. I expected company shortly: Ortiz dropping off Emily so he could give Vee his "gift." I finished my standard hot dog and Cup Noodles dinner as the sun set and realized that maybe I wasn't babysitting tonight.

I stepped back outside into dusk. The thyme had been looking droopy. I went to the house and squeaked on the hose spigot. A shuttered window offered a view inside.

Penny had a case of the zoomies. She bolted through the living room, stopping in front of Ortiz, then Vee, then Emily, barking happily. Emily chucked a tennis ball for her, which Penny caught and then dropped so she could sprint off again. Emily screeched, and Ortiz and Vee couldn't stop laughing at *that*.

A pang rippled through me.

A laughing kid, a scampering dog, two smiling parents in the warm light. It looked like a scene from a Hallmark movie, except browner. I hadn't even known about their existence for the entire first year I knew the man. I think he'd been waiting to tell me until he saw a light at the end of the tunnel—a real chance to leave the Sureños. And now he had.

I didn't have what he did. That was fine. After 22 firefighting applications, I finally had a bite. My interview with Kern County Station 37 was at 10 am. The county where the Prince Fire was currently burning. They needed every pair of hands they could get—and mine had skill and experience.

This is my time.

If I didn't get this one, I'd get the next one, or the one after that. I'd protect homes and lives, and maybe I'd even run into Kamilah out there, and we'd be wildland firefighters together. She'd see I was *good*. And then, who knows…

CHAPTER TWO

I didn't sleep much. There was a possum under the motorhome, scratching and making a *tsk* sound like a disapproving aunt, and there was a hummingbird in my chest, fluttering against my ribcage. I tried to burn off the nerves with exercise and doubled my morning run to four miles. That and the sit-ups, push-ups, and squats only calmed the hummingbird for the length of my shower.

I agonized over my beard for twenty minutes. The tattoo artist I was with before I went away, Michelle, had told me that I looked hot with a short beard. She said the dark brown hair outlined my features, "like those beautiful eyes." Hazel eyes, I've been told. That was a selectable option when you get your driver's license, but it struck me as vain, so mine just says BRN. Finally deciding, I zipped off my beard—I looked more respectable clean-shaven. It was the face of a good man. *Fake it 'til you make it.*

I dedicated five minutes to stretching and massaging my right hand, which routinely bothered me with its aches and unfinished tattoo. It wasn't bothering me now. I had my eyes on a framed letter on the wall written in a kid's scrawl. Written by the boy I'd saved while posing as a wildland firefighter. "When I grow up, I want to be a fireman like you."

Soon, Troy, I thought.

Wearing a button-up, a tie, and brand-new shoes, I rode out to meet Parole Agent Jasmine Boone at a Starbucks with time to spare. My nerves were energizing enough, so I got a coffee for her and sipped water while I waited.

I heard her before I saw her. Whistling a peppy tune, Boone strolled into the coffee shop. She was a petite but toned twenty-something with almond-colored skin. She wore her usual black polo, khakis, and a belt with a gun and radio.

"How's my favorite absconsion risk?" she greeted me.

She actually thinks she's funny, I marveled. Forcing what I called my "CalFire inmate hand crew honor grad smile," I took a folder out of my backpack and handed it over.

"I made the revisions," I said.

"First, coffee," she said, putting the folder down.

I held out the coffee I'd ordered. "Almond milk and stevia, right?"

Boone narrowed her eyes.

"Didn't you roofie a CalFire officer for one of your felony escapes?"

It'd been Ambien, and I hadn't even been charged with that particular crime, but word must've gotten around. I took a big sip and smacked my lips.

"Happy?"

She took the coffee and opened the folder to read my resume.

"And I don't have herpes."

"I know that, Jonesy."

My jaw tightened. Hated *that*. During our first meeting she'd told me I couldn't call her Jazz, but she could call me *Jonesy*? I hated that she'd seen my medical records too. She had to know which drugs were allowed to show up in my piss. Clearly, if she knew about the no-charges-pressed Ambien incident, then she knew a number of regrets that *weren't* in my rap sheet. Basically, she knew way too much about me for a woman I wasn't fucking. Not that I would. She was a good-looking lady, but everything about her was like a cheese grater on sunburned skin.

Boone rested her chin on a fist and stared at the paper. I hadn't realized my resume was worthy of such deep thinking.

"How do you get a guy to understand it's never going to happen?" she asked.

I fought to keep a *wtf* scrunch off my face and scratched my chin.

"It's that… We had a moment 'once upon a time,'" she went on, doing air quotes (*ugh*), "but that time is past."

"This seems way too personal…" *for a conversation with your parolee*, I thought. Then I thought harder: better to stay on her good side. I continued: "…for eight in the morning. But let's do it. So, this guy. You can't ghost him?"

"This isn't some guy from a dating app. Kevin and I've been through real stuff together… Interagency training, we did long distance for a while… This is someone who's important to me."

I thought of how Kamilah had ended things with me. I'd been recovering in the hospital after using my back as a bullet sponge to protect her and her cop brother. She told me I'd done a good thing, but that it didn't make me a good man. "That's a choice you have to make day-in, day-out." As for seeing me again, she'd said, "Maybe…someday…"

She'd said it to let me down easy. Her kiss on the forehead had been the nail in the coffin. I thought it could be unnailed. If I got work as a wildland firefighter, I'd be a good man, day-in, day-out, and that someday could be *one day.*

A loud sip from Boone snapped me back to reality. If her guy Kevin thought there was a chance, he could hold onto it forever.

"Be real with him. Be understanding, but be clear," I told her.

Boone nodded. It was obvious advice, but it was all I had. My gaze strayed back to the resume. Noticing, she returned her attention to it for a few seconds and waggled her head vaguely.

"It's a quick read, at least," she said, handing the resume back.

That's it? I'd spent two weeks on this thing. It was my first ever resume. It didn't have a lot on it, but it was a paper culmination of my work toward legit-ness. I clenched and unclenched my fists beneath the table.

"There was a change in your pay slips. What's going on there?"

I'd given a block of shifts away for Ortiz and I's life-changing trip, but I couldn't admit to such a massive parole violation. "Had to give up some shifts for the apartment hunt," I lied.

"Those look new," Boone said, peering at my shoes. "Five finger discount?"

"Paid for 'em myself," I said honestly, driving my knuckles into my thighs. Always trying to nail me.

"Good. Let's go," she said, tapping something on her phone. Probably noting the time of departure for her paperwork. I left my Ducati in the lot and got in the backseat of her sedan. The only way I could *legally* leave LA County was under her supervision, so I gritted my teeth to her music—speedcore is the worst—and mentally prepped for my interview.

We made it to the station house ten minutes early. It was quiet and seemingly empty. Probably all working the Prince. I checked myself in one of Boone's mirrors. The Windsor wasn't great, but it'd taken me an hour to get this knot before my parole hearing and had almost made me late. I wasn't keen to try again.

"Good luck," Boone said.

Making my way inside, the only thing stiffer than my awkward steps was my collar; it chafed against my neck, constricting. I found the only firefighter in the place, and he directed me to the engine bay.

We had to do this *here*?

A cold sweat enveloped me as I walked in. The walls of the engine bay pushed in, my collar becoming a noose.

Can't breathe.

I inhaled the strong tang of oil and gasoline. A good smell. A safe smell. The tool cabinet I grabbed like a life raft was cold and solid. The walls weren't closing in. I *could* breathe.

Whatever asshole was running the universe had a sick sense of humor. I was almost killed in a bay just like this one. To get the job, I had to put on my best performance while reliving the time two bruisers wrapped me in a carpet burrito and left me to suffocate from engine exhaust. *Should I ask to move the interview?*

No. *If you survived attempted murder, you can survive a job interview.* And if I was going to work here, I'd be in this engine bay all the time. I straightened out the now crinkled and bent folder and forged ahead.

Breathing deep, I announced myself to Chief Cisneros. He was squatting by Engine #2, in cargo pants and a Kern County Fire t-shirt. He was tall, wiry, with thick pink scars interrupting the hair on his forearms. I took note without staring. Once I built a rapport with him, maybe we could swap scar stories. I had plenty of those.

"George Cisneros." I shook his smudged hand and he apologized. "Sorry, replacing the alternator." It seemed like his thoughts were elsewhere.

The four batteries and their cables were pristine, so if he wasn't getting a full charge, it was the right call. I wished he was doing something wrong so I could show off my usefulness.

"I don't mind at all. I like the informal interview thing," I said.

He frowned and motioned to a step stool.

"Pop a squat."

I did, wary of the strained look on his face.

"Mason… Mace?"

"Mason," I replied, and held out my page of legit-ness. "Here's my resume."

"This isn't an interview," Cisneros said. He didn't take the resume.

My stomach lurched. I fought to keep my outer shell calm and polite.

"I'm doing you a favor. I understand you've been applying to a lot of engines and I wanted to save you some time and energy." Cisneros danced around before landing the uppercut. "It's just not going to happen for you."

I was floored.

"What do you mean?"

"It's not going to happen…*anywhere*. You seem like a go-getter, and you have a solid resume considering your history…but we've gained some insight on that history. More than the records provide."

While assigned to an inmate hand crew, I'd posed as a professional wildland firefighter named Pete McLean to hunt down my brother's killer, Grayson Graham. I'd confronted him, and our absence from our inmate crews might have tipped the scales toward Ash River's destruction. *Might* have. Whether it did or not was a question that kept me up at night, for the cold voice to whisper its promises of an empty life. But I'd also survived a burnover, saved a kid, and learned how it felt to protect instead of destroy.

"Okay… I—I understand. I'll tell you everything about it, how it brought me here, and why it makes me perfect for this job."

His face told me it was a lost cause.

"I don't think so. I'm sorry. Stephen Edwards, one of my best guys, came from the inmate program. So I know how it can be."

Skeevy Steve? That perverted beanpole was one of his best guys? It'd be funny if I wasn't so let down.

"This insight. Where'd it come from?"

He was silent. Didn't want to betray his source.

"C'mon. I was a non-violent offender," I told him, stomach

souring at the statement. Legally speaking, true, it was a lie in spirit. My prison sentence had been for grand larceny, but when I'd confronted Graham, I'd hacked off some fingers and beat him within an inch of his life. But it was pride in the honest sweat of this work that turned me from violence. "Maybe it's something I can make right. That's what I'm trying to do here."

"Mark Hallenbeck spoke with a few of us." He left it at that.

Hallenbeck. The night I'd abandoned my inmate crew, he had tracked me down and interrupted my beating of Graham. Graham had bashed his head with a mallet and ran.

I offered Cisneros my hand, forcing a smile as my insides constricted.

"Thanks. I appreciate your time."

I slouched into Boone's car. She studied me in the rearview.

"It can't have been that bad," she said.

I grunted.

She was still trying to cheer me up as she pulled onto the highway. "You'll get 'em next time."

I would, because this was fixable. I just had to go to the source.

CHAPTER THREE

The sign for the Merced County line whipped past and I twisted the throttle, accelerating into the last leg of another massive parole violation. I'd already barreled through three other counties outside the one I was confined to, so there was no point in turning back now. Ortiz had given me Hallenbeck's address so I could send him a Christmas card. Now I wished I had.

Boone had said no to a supervised visit to Hallenbeck. I'd tried to explain that it was important for my firefighting job search, but she smelled trouble. Did she really think I'd attack my old foreman?

It was insane. Thirty-four different applications, $4,200 dollars and three months for EMT training, and it didn't matter how much I was busting my ass because Hallenbeck was poisoning the well. Telling every firefighting commander in California that I couldn't be trusted. It was Graham who bashed in his head, not me. Hallenbeck shouldn't even have *been* there. Wrong place, wrong time.

Except that was bullshit. I hadn't been where I was supposed to be and Hallenbeck had tracked me to the Tapo Mine scar. Where I'd been about to kill my brother's murderer. I was supposed to be marching to the fireline with La Cuenca Inmate Crew Nine, protecting the town of Ash River. My stomach churned in a jarring mimicry of the engine.

The speedometer was at 140 and climbing. *Throttle control, Mason, Jesus.* I eased back. If I got pulled over for speeding, I'd end up in Merced County Jail tonight, and then back in prison.

Pulling up to his house, I had to concentrate to maintain control. My feet wanted to bounce off the bike and I was sure my hands would be shaking if they weren't tight on the handlebars. I parked in the driveway and took off my helmet for some fortifying breaths.

The house was a standard, boring Californian structure in a standard, boring Californian neighborhood. Red mission tile roofing. Stucco walls. Two-car garage. I expected something more unique from the guy who told us how inmates could lose limbs with a twinkle in his eye.

He'd probably heard me pull in…unless he wasn't home. Or what if he wasn't alone? I knew he had a wife…and I thought maybe a kid? I checked my phone: 5:45 pm. I could be interrupting dinner. Facing a cold-blooded killer seemed easier than this, and I'd done that once or twice. We were both victims of Grayson Graham, a murderer and arsonist. I had to get him to see that.

I marched to the door and tapped it with what I hoped was a polite knock. The door muffled a female voice and what sounded like my old boss's gruff tone, and then the door creaked open. A petite woman with red, graying hair and deep laugh lines stood between me and the inside of the house. There was no laughter in her eyes as she looked me up and down. Hallenbeck's wife.

"Hi, I was hoping to see Mark. I'm Mason Jones."

Mrs. Hallenbeck's eyes narrowed for a split second before she forced a polite façade. From somewhere in the house, Hallenbeck barked, "Okay."

"I'm Rita. I'll take you to him," she said, and I followed her through an antique-heavy living room to a hallway lined with family pictures featuring Hallenbeck, Rita, and a son who grew from a toddler to a college student as the hall went on. The air-conditioning tickled the sweat across my scalp, cooling my skin but not my nerves. Quiet, Rita led me to what was clearly his office, a cozy space with a desk made of golden-brown wood and matching shelves filled with books. *Ghosts of the Fireground*, *That Wild Country*, *Call Sign Chaos*, and others on similar subjects. The wildland firefighting memoirs and outdoorsy works were no surprise, but the military books were. It was all watched over by the sightless gaze of an elk head mounted on the wall. From his dim, screen-lit post behind the desk, Captain Mark Hallenbeck probed me with his eyes.

"It's an office, not a cave," Rita said, opening blinds on the window, and Hallenbeck grunted in annoyance. The finished wood took on a warm glow.

"You need your Vitamin D. Now, drinks?"

"Beer…please," Hallenbeck said. "Nothing for him… He's not staying." His speech was slow and strained. A neurological effect of the injury, I figured. A pang stirred in my chest.

Rita raised her eyebrows and glided out.

Hallenbeck grimaced at the light and stood up, a tremor in his hand as he reached to grip the desk for support. With heavy steps, he went to a chair in the corner, out of the direct light and in the shade of the mounted elk's head. The antlers edged his body in gnarled shadows. His mustache was still thick, and his face had regained the look of corn-fed fullness I'd noticed the first time I met him. But the shadows couldn't hide the snow-white spot of hair on the side of his head, or that the twinkle in his eye he'd had guiding us through the hazards of the fireline was gone. Hallenbeck sat and waited for me to speak.

I rode 250 miles to get here, but now I had a hard time meeting his gaze, and not just because of the jabberwocky shadows crisscrossing it. In a recessed shelf where the sunlight couldn't reach, a wooden shadow box languished in the gloom. It held a combat knife, silver marksmanship badges, rows and columns of military ribbons, and a plaque that dedicated it all to Staff Sergeant Mark Hallenbeck, USMC. That explained the military-interest books. It explained a lot, actually.

"I wanted to talk this out man to man," I began. *Instead of a goddamn whisper campaign.*

"At least…you're…not a coward." His speech may have been slow, but it was far from soft. He shook his head, as if to dismiss his observation as irrelevant, and pawed his cell phone over to him.

Anxiety tingled up the back of my neck.

"What are you doing?"

"You're in violation…of your parole." He painstakingly tapped in his unlock code.

"Are you serious? Haven't you done enough?"

"Haven't you?"

His scornful squint was like a shiv to the gut.

Rita interrupted a painful silence, returning with a bottled beer for her husband and a glass of water for me. He frowned at the water but said nothing. She shot her husband a mock scowl over his retreat from the sunlight, and he gave her a winning smile that she couldn't help but return.

"Why don't you take a seat?" she asked me.

Hallenbeck's smile was gone in an instant, the unfiltered disgust in his eyes making me tiny. Even though I was standing and he was sitting, he towered over me.

"Like he said, I'm not staying," I replied.

Rita shook her head and left again.

Reaching for the beer, Hallenbeck's hand seemed to fight for every inch, his arm stiff, his fingers struggling to extend. Dangerously close to knocking over the bottle, he grunted, got hold of it, and sipped. *Should he be drinking beer?* I wondered, then prickled with shame at the thought. *Guy should drink as much beer as he wants.* He returned his attention to his phone, which had re-locked. He typed in his code again.

"Captain, please."

"I'm not a captain. Not any…more," he spat. "I can't even trust myself to hold onto a hand tool. It takes me…five minutes to say a sentence…in a job where lives hang on seconds." A brittle smile cracked Hallenbeck's face. "Four deployments. The Korengal Valley. And I got my TBI…here in California from your inmate friend."

My friend?

"He killed my brother, and almost me." *Asshole.* It was a shitty thing for him to say, but if I was going to get him on my side, I'd need to use honey, not vinegar. "I know my hands aren't clean. I am sorry for what happened to you." I had apologized before, in the hospital. How many times did I have to say it?

"The things you're saying to captains and station commanders—I'm not saying you don't have a right," I went on, "but you never said it to *me*. I could've worked on it. I could've been prepared. But instead you went behind my back."

"Behind *your* back? Someone asks me…about a candidate, I answer them. Honestly." Some words and sentences he slogged through, but others spilled out like machine gun fire. "You went behind all our backs on your murder mission."

"And now I'm trying to make up for it. Doing this work is how I do that. It makes sense. I'm good at it."

"You had…a second chance and pissed on it. You want…me to give you a third?"

My face burned. I knew I'd made mistakes, but *fuck* he made me feel so small.

"Yeah," I replied. There was no point in beating around the bush.

"Honesty. Must…be hard for you." Hallenbeck's lips almost turned up. He sipped his beer and went thoughtfully quiet. Finally, he spoke. "Erik Marshall."

Erik Marshall was the man who'd paid Grayson Graham to start wildfires all over California to get leverage in a multi-billion-dollar housing development deal. His Patchwork Fire had been the deadliest and most destructive fire complex in California history. What did he have to do with me wanting another chance?

"Not…public yet, but they're going to…drop the charges against him," Hallenbeck said.

The world shifted under my feet. I finally sat down.

"How do you know?"

"Friend at the AG's…office."

"What about Wolfe?" He was a wildland firefighter who'd tried to kill me—twice. The first time was the engine bay attack. Couldn't the authorities leverage Wolfe somehow?

"Sean?" Hallenbeck used his first name. They used to work together, I remembered. "Probably hiding…in a cabin in the Cascades." He waved dismissively, the effort making his hand twitch through the shadows.

There had to be something tying Marshall to the Patchwork infernos, didn't there?

"The law…failed with Marshall. That son of a bitch. Maybe it'll…take a son of a bitch to destroy him."

"What does that mean?" I knew exactly what he meant, but I wanted him to *say it*.

He didn't answer the question. Instead, he started talking about Graham. "When I found out…you let the man that did this to me live…you should be glad I was laid up. But then he flipped."

While I was serving the remainder of my sentence at La Cuenca Conservation Camp, Graham had flipped to save his own skin. Making a deal with the DA: reduced charges in exchange for his statements on the man who hired him. Thanks to a major piece of evidence, a recording *I'd made* with Kamilah and LASD Deputy Richard Martin. Hallenbeck failed to mention that, but I decided not to interrupt him.

"I thought...maybe Inmate Jones was onto something. Maybe what Rita says, what God says, about forgiveness...maybe it's right. But he flipped back. Re...tracted his statements. Clammed up like...a virgin at a whorehouse."

The ground ripped away under my feet. Graham flipped back? I'd done the right thing—cooperated with an LASD deputy, got the evidence, even *saved Graham's life*. And it had worked out to the good! The world fell out of focus. *What the fuck what the fuck what the fuck.*

I'd stayed away from the details of the investigation. I got the occasional email or phone call from detectives about my statement, and helpful hints from Richard, but I kept my distance. I didn't want to know.

I was falling through darkness. This couldn't be happening. *I was on a new path.*

"Which brings us...back to you," Hallenbeck said. The man and his study came back into focus.

"You want me to take on Erik Marshall?"

"To destroy him."

"I'm not a killer."

"You're not." He seemed disappointed. "Not...what I'm asking. Do what you do best. Lie, cheat, and steal. Destroy...his *world*."

I'm on a new path.

"So, your sales pitch here is, 'Hey, you're a piece of shit. Go forth and be a piece of shit for the right reasons.'"

Hallenbeck's shrug said, *Basically, yeah.*

Fire burned from my face to my fists. Trying to fight it, I clutched the condensation-slick water Rita had left me, almost dropping it as I bolted down a gulp.

"I already did that. That's what got me into the mess you won't let me clean up."

"You weren't…doing it for the right reasons," Hallenbeck scoffed.

He had me there. But this was some hypocritical bullshit.

"You had every fire chief in California turn me away because of all the bad shit I did, but if I do bad shit for *you,* then you'll give me your blessing?"

"Not for me. Erik Marshall has money and power. Way more…dangerous than you." So I was as much of a piece of shit as him, but poor. Awesome. "And no," Hallenbeck continued, "it's not in ex…change for my blessing. The men and women working fires need to be able to trust each other. You don't belong out there."

"Well, then yeah, *of course* I'll take on this guy, what with all the danger and chance of going back to prison it entails. You're offering such a sweet deal." I ran my hands through my hair and sighed. Insanity. He was asking me to fly to the moon on a bicycle.

"Think of it…as restitution. Not money. Real restitution. You bring down…Marshall, I'd say that earns you a clean slate."

"A clean slate?"

"In the…cosmic sense."

"Goodbye, Mark," I said. I murmured thanks to Rita as I left his house in a daze, face smoldering, a concrete slab in my chest. Taillights and highway signs became a blur as I throttled back to Los Angeles. This wasn't the Hallenbeck that I'd looked up to. This was someone else.

I hated him.

CHAPTER FOUR

Nick Curione

-2140-
-END-TO-END ENCRYPTION ACTIVE-

NC: Jones broke parole again. Tracked to Mark Hallenbeck's residence. Images attached. MH was GG assault victim, CalFire captain at La Cuenca Conservation Camp.

EM: Any other details?

NC: Not yet. At his parole agent's office now to see what she knows.

EM: Keep me posted.

NC: Always, sir.

At 9:40 pm, the third floor of the Division of Adult Parole Operations building was dark and empty, save one man. Slender and sinewy with a shock of fully, prematurely gray hair, the man's North American alias was Nick Curione. He inserted a thumb drive in Jasmine Boone's computer and its tiny LED strobed. It usually took about ten minutes to do its thing.

While it did, Curione went through her cubicle. His fingertips were armored by nitrile gloves and his eyes were aided by the soft light of an egg-shaped night-light. It was made for babies, but it fit these kinds of missions perfectly.

Kinder chocolate bars, water flavoring packets, a sports bra, and deodorant. A picture of her tabby cat. No jotted numbers or handwritten notes. The 27-year-old's cubicle didn't have a single piece of physical intel. He'd have to rely on her digital workspace. The fixer eyed the rapidly blinking LED—still hoovering.

Beep. That sound didn't come from the thumb drive or computer. It was a keycard entry on this floor. Curione shrank to a crouch but left the egg light on—a change in lighting snagged the mind more than a dim glow.

Click. The office lights came on, overpowering the tiny light anyway. He blinked rapidly, eyes adjusting. Footsteps and the rattle of plastic wheels. Probably a janitor.

The fixer checked his tactical watch. 2146. He checked the thumb drive: still blinking. The cubicle's sliding door was open, and Curione doubted he could close it quietly. He heard the clunk of bins being emptied and the rustle of thin plastic. Definitely a janitor. It was too bad they hadn't finished their third-floor tasks earlier.

He took out a coiled wire with hand-worn grips. A clay cutter, but the fixer had never used it for that purpose. Maybe the janitor wouldn't pass this way, but if they did, Curione would be ready.

Marshall would not accept a glimmer of exposure. That was why Curione was here.

L ater, Curione sat in his unremarkable sedan on a secluded hill beneath the stars. Neat rows of stone slabs caught the moonlight, but he was focused on the glowing laptop on his thighs. The thumb drive was inserted, Boone's local and network files arrayed onscreen in neat rows not unlike those outside his car. He made his report.

DAPO files pose little to no risk. Incidental mention of you and GG in early meetings. Nothing recently. Nothing new to report.

He signed out of the encrypted messaging app and got to more pressing business. Putting on a fresh pair of gloves, he opened the trunk. Bleach, shovel, and the janitor's corpse ready for him.

The dead man's bloodshot eyes were stuck open in his stupid purple face. Curione hadn't enjoyed it. It wasn't like Botswana or Libya, where some tangoes presented a real challenge. You really had to apply your skillset in a mission like that. This man? This man was a blip.

And now he had to dig up a recent grave and put this blip in it. Curione didn't enjoy that either. But damn if the money wasn't good.

CHAPTER FIVE

Tsk, tsk, tsk. Tsk, tsk, tsk. The possum under the motorhome clicked throughout the night. A quick search online told me it meant that it was a male trolling for a mate. *We're all lonely, dude. And some of us are trying to sleep.*

The next day, I bought a possum trap and laid out the wire walls in the back yard. Once it was put together, it'd be a non-lethal cage that I could use to move the little bastard elsewhere. I'd ask Ortiz about that—he worked at an animal shelter. Maybe the bait would even attract a female for him, and they could live happily ever after.

If I could get the damn thing *together*. The hooks didn't reach the links where I thought they attached, and I kept getting an A-frame that collapsed into a jumble of aluminum. Was there a YouTube video for the assembly? Yes. Was I going to use it? No. I was a construction worker. *I should be able to figure this out.*

When I couldn't, I just laid down in the grass and stared at the sky. The motorhome door wasn't latched and it banged in the wind. Getting up and shutting it was too much work though.

Bang. Bang. Bang.

Like someone in a huff pounding on a door. Like Kit in a huff pounding on the door of Caleb and I's place in Torrance almost 11 years ago.

I'd been 19. She was out of a stint in rehab and wanted to see her sons. Caleb had caught wind of the visit from Jenny and made himself scarce, but he said I should hear her out. I think he knew it was a Step Nine visit. Caleb had cooled on her by then. A lot, actually. Once upon a time, he'd seen her as a victim. He'd even come up with a plan to free Kit from her dealer, Rick. We would steal meth from the cook and pin it on the dealer. That had gone to shit. It ended up with Rick cornering us in an abandoned oil field, a shotgun aimed at my face. Caleb had tackled him, stabbed him in the eye, and sliced his throat to stop the screaming. After we buried him, Caleb had expected a miraculous turnaround. Kit just found another dealer. She didn't know what we'd done for her, but all the same, when she threw that chance away, it had broken him.

She showed up at the doorstep, apple-cheeked and chubby. Guess they fed her well at the center. It irked me. The least she could do was have the decency to look chewed-up. That and a medallion she showed me seemed to prove that she wasn't using. At the moment. I wouldn't put a penny on her staying clean. She saw Caleb was absent and cursed Jenny for reaching out. I allowed her to hug me. I remember the wheeze of her windbreaker as I limply touched her back.

Like Caleb suspected, Kit was there to make amends. She held an ink-stained piece of paper in shaking hands and sniffled through the words written there—all the things she was sorry for. How her drug use made our home "unstable" and that no kid should have to go through what we did. "I know that, as a mother, I haven't—"

I stopped her there.

"No need," I said. "Things are the way they should be." There wasn't a tremor in my voice. There wasn't a lump in my throat. There *wasn't.*

She burst into tears and asked to come inside. I think Caleb would have let her in, and that's why he stayed away. He may have cooled on her, but he still saw her as his mother. I shut the door.

She screamed and cursed and pounded it. *Bang bang bang.* "I'm your mother! Macie, goddammit, let me in! I'm your mother!" Her voice screeched and cracked. The door rattled on its hinges. I perched on the edge of the couch, stewing. I'd made the right decision, but it didn't keep my face from heating or my vision from blurring. I refused to engage. A neighbor slammed a window open and threatened to call the cops. She sobbed and finally plodded away.

After that, she left a voicemail or texted every few years, and Caleb or I texted back that things were fine.

Funny thing. When Caleb was murdered and I was laid up and could've used a word from Mom, I didn't hear a fucking peep.

Bang. Bang. Click.

Ortiz latched the motorhome door closed and sauntered over to me. I was still face-up in the grass, and I could see that the shaving line of his beard scruff was uneven under his chin.

"Heartache or fartache?" he asked, which was our version of *What's wrong?* It had started when Ortiz was having some major stomach issues—which I think were because of his guilt over hiding his secret family from me.

I told him about the interview and what Hallenbeck had done. I didn't mention his batshit offer or that I was thinking about my mom for no damn reason.

"Damn, bro."

Exactly. He understood, and it gave me a flicker of energy. I sat up.

"I just want to be like that farmer guy, you know, the one from the meme? 'It ain't much, but it's honest work'?"

"Trust."

"The farmer dude is happy because he has a job that's perfect for him."

"Nah. He's happy because he accepts what he has."

Agree to disagree, I thought. I wondered if there was an asshole in tweed at some hoity-toity college getting paid a boatload to teach a class on meme interpretation. I bet there was.

"Let's finish that tequila," Ortiz said.

"Maybe later." Self-medicating was Kit's thing. It had been Caleb's too. I avoided it like the plague. I made a show of getting back to work on the possum trap and Ortiz left me to it.

It ain't much, but it's honest work.

When I let go of my rage over Caleb's death and finally mourned him, it had hollowed me out. The dusty work of firebreaks and erosion control had filled me back up. Shit-talking and joking with the crew. The scent of woodsmoke and tree sap, blue skies and starry nights. The knowledge that you're doing something that matters. I wasn't ready to give up on firefighting. I *was* done with this goddamn trap.

I called up Jeff Nelson, who'd I worked under after the Ash River fiasco. Nelson worked on the Incident Command side now, connecting him to National Parks and Forestry. It wasn't likely that wildland crews at the federal level would give me a chance, but I had to check. He tried and failed to put lipstick on the pig that was my situation…all while confirming it.

I was blacklisted.

So I went back to my life of construction work, hot dogs, and ramen. I'd like to say that I stayed positive, but I don't con people anymore. Especially myself. First I stopped doing my morning run, then I stopped doing sit-ups, push-ups, and squats. What was the point?

Days became weeks.

I wasn't a complete shitbag. I fixed up the motorhome, which was the pretextual exchange of services Ortiz had okayed in return for a break on rent. I cleaned the spark plugs and replaced the ignition switch, fuel pump, and fuel line to get the engine running. I kept going. Cleaning, replacing, tuning. Under the hood every day to keep the madness at bay.

Agent Boone tossed the place during an unscheduled visit. Trying to nail me again, but this time it didn't bother me. As I waited outside, I saw her pull Troy's framed letter off the wall and look it over. Then she looked at me. *That* bothered me. I was an ape in a fiberglass tree watching its zookeeper study it, wondering why it'd been throwing shit at the glass. My teeth clicked. *Stop grinding your teeth, Mason.*

She finished her search and got to the questions. Had I been in contact with any associates from my past? I hadn't. Was I staying clean? That'd never been a problem for me. Was I keeping up with my bills? As best I could. Hadn't she seen the ramen and hot dogs? Apparently, Hallenbeck hadn't reported my excursion, because she didn't bring it up. That should've been a relief.

When she left, everything felt out of place, but nothing was. Troy's framed letter put a pit in my chest, so I put it in the cupboard.

Weeks became months.

I moved my herbs from planters to pots. Ortiz told me Vee was pregnant. Buzzed from a celebration with her family, he cackled about the date of conception. "I told you I was gonna put another baby in her!" Another huge life step for my buddy. My brain registered his joy and that I was supposed to feel it too. I wanted to be happy for him, but I was numb. I forced a grin and pounded his fist with mine. "Dude, congratulations! That's great." The words were as hollow as I was. Maybe I wasn't done conning people.

More months passed. I got discharged from parole. Boone shook my hand. "Be safe, be smart, stay out of trouble." I became a totally free man, legally speaking, and Ortiz demanded celebration. I declined. It didn't matter. My life wasn't changing.

On a Tuesday no different from any other, I bent over the trench I was digging behind the green-meshed MTS Construction fence. The excavator had been through and now me and a gang of orange-shirted workers were prepping it for a concrete pour. The other men held an animated debate on the merits of *tetas vs. culo*. I was lost in my thoughts.

This was a lot like scraping a fireline. Manual labor out in the sun. I wore orange there too. The sweat drips the same, water vanishing in the heat and salt baking into the dirt. This sweat could be spent building shields of earth to protect people's homes, instead of it building yet another cluster of luxury apartments.

On my first break, I read a text from an unknown number.

It's Kamilah, this is not spam.

It came with a link to an article from the *Sacramento Bee*. I tapped it.

"Judge dismisses all charges against real estate developer in alleged arson plot."

The fact that Kamilah had texted me—which was always the first event in an elaborate fantasy that ended with us coming home to each other and a big scruffy mutt from Ortiz's shelter—barely registered.

Hallenbeck hadn't been fucking with me.

Did that mean he was right about the other part? That it takes a son of a bitch to destroy one?

A clean slate.

The ravings of a man consumed by rage. I knew better than to listen to it—I'd been there myself. *So forget it.*

I got back to digging and tried to forget about Hallenbeck's offer.

I failed. Could he be right? The state of California believed in restitution. Half of every dollar I'd made as an inmate crewman had gone to court-ordered restitution. Judge Taglianetti's direct order said I owed Mercedes Benz $200,000, and I'd been chipping away at that amount since the day I was sentenced. Eventually, you pay it back. Eventually, you can make up for it.

A clean slate.

Not a record getting legally expunged. Not court-ordered commutation. Not a good deed but a great deed, doing something that would silence that voice forever. The conversation was months ago, but now it dominated my thoughts. Like a phrase that brings a shitty pop song to the forefront of your mind, the chorus ringing over and over and over again. A mind worm. Had he meant that to happen?

A clean slate.

CHAPTER SIX

I kicked out the stand and hopped off my bike at the Del Rio scenic overlook. When I flipped up the visor of my helmet, a breeze tickled my eyelashes and the brightness pounded my eyes. Rolling hills rippled out from the river that gave the area its name, green with vines and orange with workers plucking grapes. A building complex stood on the tallest hill in the landscape. Redhorn Winery, owned by Erik Marshall.

Before today, I'd known very little about the man who hired my brother's killer to set California ablaze. The topic had been radioactive, bricked off like Chernobyl. Despite the sun, my leather jacket, and the engine heat baked into the legs of my jeans, I was cold. Did I really want to bore into Chernobyl?

I thought about what I'd learned as I rode up to the winery. As a prominent real estate developer, there was a lot to be found online. He was dismissed from the Spear Company when the charges against him appeared—with a big severance package. The ol' golden parachute. Now he did something with private equity and algorithmic trading. I didn't know what that was, just that it kept him rich. Son of an engineer and businessman. Bill Marshall, founder of the Marshall Corporation. Born into money. Because of course he was.

I parked the bike again and a gorgeous hostess took me to an open-air tasting room. The view from the tasting area was incredible, and so was everything else about the property. My waiter showed up in moments, a sharp-eyed dude named Liam. My jeans were a dusty husk with ratty hems. My scar-riven, unfinished tattoo prickled in the sun. And I probably had helmet hair up the wazoo. I did not belong here.

I ordered a pinot noir because of a movie I'd seen. It wasn't for me—just tasted like sour grape juice. I wondered if I could get a beer or whiskey instead, and if I could return the pinot noir without paying for it. Probably a *no* on both counts.

On top of this being a working winery, Marshall had a home on this estate. It looked like a manor and it was visible from my table. Within sniping distance, I couldn't help but notice. But no one seemed to be home, and as Hallenbeck had rightly pointed out, I wasn't a killer.

Marshall also had addresses in Aspen, France, and the Caribbean. Summer homes, winter homes, vacation homes. Homes for days. And a superyacht. All that money, all that *luxury…* It was a slap in the face to those whose homes had burned down because of him. To those who had *died* because of him.

"Sir, are you all right?"

Liam the waiter's worried voice brought me out of my thoughts. I'd snapped the stem of the glass and spilled wine all over the table. He rushed over with a napkin and I caught the bulb of the glass as it toppled over the lip.

"Here, it's my mess," I said, motioning for the cloth as he sopped up the purple-red liquid.

"No no, it's my job. I don't want you to cut yourself again."

Sure enough, there was a slice on my index finger dribbling bright crimson spots into the napkin.

"Shit, man, I'm sorry," I said.

Gracious and understanding, Liam assured me everything was okay, cleaned up the table, and brought me a first aid kit for the cut.

It was hard to believe this place was owned by a heartless murderer.

"Destroy his world," Hallenbeck had said.

How? By tearing down his empire using my skills as a liar and a thief?

Gritting my teeth, I rinsed the cut with water, applied antibiotic gel from the kit, and wrapped a bandage around the finger.

I could steal from the winery. But then they'd just cut costs. Reduce hours and lay off workers. When you steal from a business, you're never sticking it to the people at the top. It's always the people at the bottom, like Liam, who suffer. Back in the day, I *always* tried to steal directly from rich assholes. That's me: Mason Jones, responsible thief.

Let's say I was able to get closer to Marshall without getting made and found something deeply personal to him and stole it…

Then what? He fires some security guys, probably his maid—guy like that, *definitely* his maid—is pissed for a while…and then goes back to plundering California. So he just goes on with his untouchable existence, making wines, sitting on his ass while algorithms fill up his Scrooge McDuck money vault, jetting from one estate to the other?

What else could be done? Murder? Arson? As much as Hallenbeck wanted me to be, I wasn't that guy. There was no way to destroy Marshall without hurting others. Liam brought me a replacement glass of sour grapes. *A bit on the nose, Universe.* The sun turned droplets in the glass prismatic. It was a sight that belonged in a brochure, but it just made me want to smash it all over again. It wasn't fair.

It's not like I could get him arrested, right? Graham had recanted and apparently they didn't have sufficient evidence. That meant they'd need new evidence to bring charges against Marshall again. Or witnesses.

Hadn't Hallenbeck said something about Sean Wolfe being in the wind? Wolfe had been the one that trapped me in an engine bay to poison me with vehicle exhaust. That was the first time he'd tried to kill me. I later found out that Wolfe had been set to take a job at Spear, where Marshall had been an executive. What did he know about Marshall's crimes? If nothing else, he could testify to Marshall ordering hits on me.

If he was alive…if he could be found…if I could get him to talk…then there was a chance I could take on Marhsall the *right* way. Not the outlaw way. *If, if, if.*

CHAPTER SEVEN

Nick Curione

-1632-
-END-TO-END ENCRYPTION ACTIVE-

NC: *Jones was at Redhorn today. Had one glass of wine and left.*

EM: *When is his parole up?*

NC: *It just ended.*

EM: *That timing is extremely relevant. Should have said that up front.*

Curione spat. The boss wouldn't message again until he abased himself.

NC: Absolutely, sir. I apologize. It won't happen again.

EM: It won't. Make Jones a surveillance priority.

NC: Yes, sir. I'll handle it myself.

CHAPTER EIGHT

I went for a run for the first time in months. The sky was gloomy but fierce winds carried me on the way out. I fought them all the way back. A restaurant sign skittered down the street like a sail without a ship. Trees swayed, their leaves hissing. I jumped over a fallen branch, earning a scratch on my calf. I had energy again. My muscles screamed at me, but the fact that I'd earned the shower afterward made the drumming water more soothing.

I started to tap out a text and stopped, deciding the Starcraft needed its floors swept. Also the countertops needed dusting. Then another sweep because of all the dead skin I'd banged loose, and then a feverish wipe down of every surface. Finally, I made myself text Hallenbeck, telling him that we needed to talk.

I sat at the kitchen table in the motorhome, insisting on a videoconference so I could read his face when I asked him my questions. I was good at catching lies. I'd always thought of Hallenbeck as an honest man, but our last conversation had shattered that image.

"What did you say happened to Wolfe?" I asked.

"He's…missing," Hallenbeck said, frowning.

It was an honest answer and an honest frown. He didn't know where Wolfe was, and he wasn't happy about my interest in the man.

The passenger window rattled from the wind. What was left of its rubber seal was brittle and cracked. I really needed to fix that.

"How well did you know him?" I asked.

He sighed.

"It won't…work."

"Says who?"

"Me. If Sean…still works for Marshall, he won't talk. If he doesn't, Marshall…will have him killed. That's if he's even alive."

"Why not try? You want me to take on Marshall like I'm the Punisher or something." Thar be monsters—and the monsters are me. "I've been down that road. I won't go down it again. It's always the people at the bottom who suffer. Even if there *was* a way to hurt him without hurting others, you don't poke a bear without a bear trap on deck."

"How long did…you work on that one?"

I'd been workshopping that statement in my head since Del Rio, but I didn't dignify his question with a response. A powerful gust buffeted the motorhome and a cupboard yawned open.

"You said Wolfe is probably hiding in the Catskills?"

"Cas…cades."

"See? You know him."

"We worked…together for a minute or two," he admitted.

"He's the piece that connects Marshall and Graham. He made an official recommendation to get Graham on the fireline. He was going to take a job at the company where Marshall was an executive. If he's alive, he has damn good reason to be in the wind. What if I could find him and get him to tell the cops or FBI what he knows? I *was* a sonofabitch…so maybe I can *find* a sonofabitch."

"Maybe."

Maybe, maybe. If, if, if.

The wind howled. A siren whined in the distance. There was an energy to the idea I couldn't ignore, but it was so uncertain. It was one thing to say I could find Wolfe, and another to do it. And the more important question, one that all the wrong I'd done had taught me to consider: Should I?

I sat with Ortiz at his kitchen table, having filled him in on my idea for a Wolfe hunt. Vee was at the counter, pretending to do meal prep but actually intruding on what I'd meant to be a private conversation. She was in her second trimester and had a small baby bump. Penny was ambling back and forth under the table, alternately getting scritches from me and her dad. Emily sat in the next room watching a cartoon about a girl running around Paris with ladybug superpowers.

"What should I do?" I asked. My body crackled with energy, but also uncertainty.

"Get your own place," Vee said.

"Thanks, peanut gallery." I focused on Ortiz with a pointed

look. "You always have an opinion. What do you think?"

"You should do whatever snaps you out of this funk. Stop being a…" He stopped short.

"Pussy?" Vee scowled.

"I would never say that, *mi vida*," he replied with a sly smile. "It wouldn't even make sense. Pussies are tough as hell. How they ended up as the word for *temeroso,* I'll never understand."

Satisfied, Vee returned his sly smile, but now I was the one who was offended. I didn't know exactly what *temeroso* meant, but there's a thing called context.

"I'm not *temeroso.*"

Ortiz teased me with a dubious look.

I spun their bottle of Valentina hot sauce clockwise on the table, watching the dark orange liquid flow against the glass.

"Erik Marshall *is* a son of a bitch," I said. Innocent people had died because of the Patchwork Fire.

"He is," Ortiz agreed.

"He got away with murder." I kept the hot sauce spinning with taps of my finger.

"He did."

"So you think I should do it."

"I don't know."

"Well what the fuck? I need your advice." I stopped the bottle, making sure it wasn't pointed at my best friend or his wife. It wasn't that kind of party.

"I'm not in this fight," he said, earning an approving nod from Vee, "so it's your decision to make. I'm in therapist mode."

"Therapy for ex-cons, by ex-cons."

Ortiz smiled.

"Don't give him any ideas," Vee said.

I spun the bottle counterclockwise. What if I *could* find Wolfe and use him to fight the good fight against Marshall? Wouldn't that make up for what I'd done? Maybe, as a *former* liar and thief, I could see something the law couldn't. Maybe I could do some good *and* keep my hands clean. Clean hands, clean slate.

My pulse quickened. The idea had a crystallizing, weightless feel to it. It made me feel like skipping. I clamped my right hand on the bottle, stopping it. The muscles in it twinged, bringing my attention to the unfinished tattoo. The ink was a reminder of the rage that had defined me after Graham murdered Caleb. The rage had given me purpose. I'd rebuilt my broken body with it. Been laser-focused on Graham's downfall because of it—at the expense of everything and everyone else. It had almost consumed me.

"You okay?"

Ortiz must have seen me wince.

I wiggled my hand, and he nodded in understanding.

"Erik Marshall is connected to Graham," I said. "To go after Erik Marshall…" My stomach churned. There was something about it I couldn't get past.

"Named must your fear be, before banish it you can," Ortiz crooned in spot-on Yoda.

What *was* I afraid of?

When I saved Graham instead of letting him die, when I made my statements and gave my deposition to the glaring black eye of a camera, I'd let that rage go. Or had I just buried it?

A chill rippled up my spine, raising goosebumps on my arms.

I was afraid to dig it back up again.

So I'm letting my fears dictate my life now?

Fuck that.

I texted Hallenbeck: Send me anything you have on Wolfe. I'm going to find him.

My phone rang in response.

"I'm…coming with you," Hallenbeck said.

I t had just stopped raining, and brilliant shafts of light broke through marbled clouds. Lightning flashed on the gray-streaked horizon. Ortiz and I sat on his porch, finally polishing off the *anejo*. He gaped at the Wikipedia article on his phone.

"700 miles south to north. 80 miles wide. Almost 60,000 square miles."

"Yup." That was our search grid: the Cascade Range, which stretched from Northern California through Oregon, Washington, and into Canada.

Wolfe had told Hallenbeck he wanted to retire at some small town in the foothills—he didn't remember which or if Wolfe had even said, but there was an abandoned church there he wanted to rebuild. *Good Catholic boy that he was*, but I kept that snark internal. Ortiz was serious about that stuff.

So, if Wolfe was alive, he was in the foothills of one of 4,375 mountains. We had our work cut out for us.

"Are you sure I can take the motorhome?" I asked Ortiz. I needed him to say yes but tried to be casual. This could take weeks, maybe even months, and I didn't expect Hallenbeck to shell out for my motel expenses.

"Yeah. You're the one that got it working."

"But you gave me a break on rent for that." Negotiating against yourself is stupid, but, man, Ortiz had done so much for me already.

He waved it off.

"Thanks, man." I didn't deserve Ortiz. I wondered if he knew that.

"Are *you* sure you don't need backup?"

I flicked my eyes at the screen door. Inside, Emily was trying to teach Penny to play dead and having a hard time of it.

"Yeah, I'm sure," I said.

Grateful, he nodded and clinked my glass. We sat in the quiet, taking our time finishing off the last pour.

We went inside and I said my goodbyes.

I hugged Emily and scratched Penny's wiggly butt. Vee watched with ill-concealed satisfaction.

"Take care of yourself," I said. I held out my hand.

Vee tilted her head at that, smiling gently. She pushed my hand down and hugged me.

"You too, Mason."

Ortiz walked me to the back door.

"Call me if you need me though," he murmured.

We bro-hugged and I went out back. I knelt next to my potted herbs. Breathed in the rosemary's woody aroma. This is what I had to do, wasn't it? This was my chance, right? I brought the herbs inside the motorhome.

And now I was packed.

CHAPTER NINE

As you go north in California, the rugged yellow hills become smoother and greener. Then they retreat completely, replaced by crops marching over flat tracts that stretch for miles. Roadside stands for strawberries and garlic whip past between billboards saying *NO WATER NO JOBS* and *JESUS IS HOPE.*

Hallenbeck sat in the passenger seat, looking at actual physical maps. Old school. He hadn't said a word since we got on the road. Not about my Wu-Tang, and not about his passenger window rattling. I'd forgotten to get a new seal for it. The motorhome engine itself thrummed beautifully and the gears shifted without a hitch. The ancient transmission, with its fresh fluid and brand-new filter, was in great shape. I rummaged in the seatback pocket, found my EMT study guide, and tore off the cover. I offered it to Hallenbeck.

"Jam that in the window."

He slid the cover in the window and the rattle disappeared. He nodded at me and went back to his maps.

Frosty silence be damned—I had a *mission*. Restless energy surged over me. I wanted to put the pedal to the floor. I wanted to bounce out of my seat. I wanted to howl, *Foul, fall through, child was wild,* along with the track I was blasting.

We'd met at the Merced Walmart parking lot for a gear check and mission brief. I guessed he'd had a rideshare drop him off, because if it had been his wife, wouldn't she stay for goodbyes? Hallenbeck had been standing there with a large pack at his feet, leaning on a cane. A knot tightened in my gut. I hadn't seen him use that in his study. I knew he had physical issues because of his traumatic brain injury, but I didn't know the extent of them. If we were going to capture a Wolfe, I needed to find out. And there was something else tightening the knot. Sticking out of the rolled-up sleeping mat on his pack was the muzzle of a rifle.

I showed him a case of bottled water and a roadside kit I was bringing.

"This it?" he asked.

"The mutual stuff, yeah. I have my own, like, sundries, and aren't we doing our own things for food?"

"Bring out every…thing."

"You too," I said. "This is a partnership."

Hallenbeck knelt, grunting, and took neatly rolled items out of the pack. I threw out a blanket and we laid everything on it. I didn't hold anything back.

My propane tank and toolbox. His first aid kit and a sleeping bag.

"You planning on sleeping in the motorhome?"

He pulled out a rubber-banded roll of Benjamins. "You cover the roof overhead and I'll...cover gas and other expenses. Each responsible for our own food." His speech seemed smoother. Maybe it was better in the mornings when he was fresh?

"Works for me." It was gonna be tight quarters, but him bank-rolling the mission was a godsend—me being poor as shit. Trying to seem casual, I gave him a once-over. In the morning sun, it was easy to see the crescent-shaped, thumbnail-sized craniotomy scar beneath the white spot on his head. "Is it safe for you to drive?"

"Not supposed to."

I hope you can wipe your own ass. A shitty thought, I know. I wasn't keen on babysitting a cripple, even if it was exactly what I deserved. It would suck for *him* too... I remembered my time in the hospital with an inward twinge. It was humiliating to have to rely on someone else to clean your prison wallet. The driving limitation seemed like a natural pivot to questions about any others, but I couldn't bring myself to ask them. I didn't want to get that harsh, shrink-ray glare.

We checked each other's gear. My hygiene kit and clothes. His hygiene kit and clothes.

"More socks," he said.

"More socks?"

"More socks."

Yes sir, Mr. Marine. I went into the Walmart to buy them, plus a second case of bottled water at his urging. "You never...know," he said. "And on that note..."

He opened a survival kit. It had rope, waterproof matches, a tactical flashlight, fishing line and lures, a wire saw, clips and carabiners, a silver emergency blanket, and a flintstone. I saw a glimmer of the old twinkle in his eyes. He was proud of it.

"Yeah, it's all right," I said, and with a grin I brought out my own backpack. "These are my tricks n' treats."

Ortiz and I had put it together for our Reno-Tijuana road trip but we'd never needed anything in it. A locksmith tool, motion sensors, nitrile gloves, two projectile stun guns, a blowtorch, pepper spray, zip ties, multi-purpose grease, burner phones, a few knives, and Wolfe's own Leatherman, which I'd taken off him the second time he'd tried to kill me.

"Eh?"

"Not bad," he admitted, and unrolled the sleep mat, pulling out—stiffly—his weapon. It was a hunting rifle with a woodgrain stock.

My right hand ached, sending a creeping pulse chestward.

"Why the gun?"

"Rifle," he corrected. "Self-defense."

I massaged my palm, tempering the pulse. I wasn't sure if self-defense would hold up in California if you were going looking for trouble. I hadn't brought a lethal option—and for good reason. If we found Wolfe, I wanted to disarm and corner him. Not kill him. Hallenbeck's hands weren't steady either. What if he shot Wolfe by accident? What if he shot him on *purpose*? All that talk about the law not working and me destroying Marshall... He might want to do the same to Wolfe, his old work buddy who had betrayed him.

"The plan is to find him and talk to him, yeah?"

"That's…right," Hallenbeck said.

The plan, specifically, was this:

Step One: Find Wolfe. *Step Two*: Find out what he knows. *Step Three*: Bring in the authorities so they can leverage him against Marshall.

"What does Rita think about all this?"

"This isn't my first…hunting trip." He shrugged.

I wondered how much he'd told her. I'd suggested meeting at his house for the gear check, but he'd insisted on meeting here. I'd have to keep an eye on this guy.

"All right." I shrugged.

I thought our gearhead moment would earn us a chiller vibe, but it was still tense two hours into the trip when we passed through Sacramento.

CHAPTER TEN

Lush farms turned to forested hills and we went from the straightaway 99 to the snaky 32, reaching our first stop, Lassen Volcanic National Park, in the early afternoon. Lassen Peak was the first Cascade Mountain in the range. Looking at the map, the park covered a hundred-something square miles we could take off our search grid. There wasn't going to be an abandoned church on federal land, much less one that a wanted man would risk running into park rangers over. It was the area around it we had to search.

We ate a late lunch and Hallenbeck spread out his handiwork on the small kitchen table. On a map, he'd marked three abandoned churches in the Lassen Peak area that he'd found online.

"Let's get to it," he said.

I downed my veggie smoothie—it was time to be healthy

again—and slid back into the driver's seat.

When we pulled up to the first mark, a man was in a driveway bent over the rear-engine of a classic VW Beetle. I suppressed the urge to land a soft drive on Hallenbeck's shoulder and shout "Slug bug yellow," and instead peered extra-studiously at the building behind the car. It had a brick façade and arched windows, but it had clearly been converted into a house. There was a swing set out front, and, of course, this dude, who was now squinting at us.

"Nice Bug," I called out the window, and drove on.

The second abandoned church had been converted into a Timberline Saloon. We drove on again. The fastest route to the third was through the rugged beauty of the mountainous national park under a crisp blue sky. Oh darn. Hallenbeck was as good as his word and shelled out 80 bucks for a pass good at every national park for a year, and the winding park highway took us to the clearest water I'd ever seen—Lake Helen. The rocks beneath the crystal water sparkled, and the rocks above it, the craggy mountain peaks, made rippled reflections. The tallest one was Lassen Peak, a snowcapped volcano that had last erupted a hundred years ago. I wondered if they were like earthquakes—the longer the tension builds, the bigger the explosion.

Every parking spot was taken, so I double-parked.

"Just a sec," I told Hallenbeck.

A sign gave directions to a Lassen Peak Trail and another called:

"Bumpass Hell," I chortled, grinning at Hallenbeck.

"Good hike," he said.

"Oh yeah?"

The asshole didn't offer anything else. This was going to be a long trip.

I stepped outside and breathed it in. Visitors and hikers walked around and a kid on the shore was laughing. It smelled of sunscreen and pine. Not so long ago, I'd been so consumed with rage that I'd ignored beauty like this. I wasn't here to stop and smell the roses… but that didn't mean I couldn't someday. Once my slate was clean. When I had truly made up for all the wrong I'd done, then I could truly *live*.

I took out a small notebook I'd brought for our Wolfe hunt. I wrote down:

Hike Lassen Peak (And Bumpass Hell? lol)

Maybe I couldn't be a wildland firefighter, but I could still enjoy the wildlands. I smiled and stepped back into the motorhome.

The third mark was a wooden, single-room, Old West-looking church. Looked like more of a chapel than a church, but I wasn't an architect or a churchgoer. When we stepped out of the motorhome, I noticed Hallenbeck didn't use his cane, walking stiffly as we approached the discolored building.

"You don't need your cane?"

"No."

We peered through the cracked windows. No sign of anyone. I got a workout opening the door. It was water-warped and its hinges were fused together by rust. We padded along the creaking floorboards. A chipmunk skittered out from under a rotten pew, but there was no sign of human habitation. The church was a quiet shell.

"I'm not trying to pry. Just want to be prepared." *And thinking about what would happen if we had to literally chase after Wolfe.*

"We should…should stake it out," Hallenbeck said, side-stepping my weak-ass, Good Cop-style interrogation attempt.

"You see something I don't? There's no renovation going on here and that door hasn't been opened in years."

"Maybe. Let's…make sure."

"Roger that," I said. It wasn't a great candidate for Wolfe's fixer-upper, with no fixing going on that I could see…but it *was* our first candidate.

I placed a motion sensor above the door trim.

"Let's ask around," I said.

We went into town, a small vill called Old Station, and showed people Wolfe's picture. No one recognized him. We went back to the church and took the motorhome off-road just far enough to be out of sight. We staked it out for three days. The only activity was an owl setting off the motion sensor, probably hunting that chipmunk. We talked to the priests and pastors of a town called Burney. They didn't have any leads for us either.

Lassen Peak was a bust.

We breakfasted at a picnic table supported by wagon wheels instead of legs. Rentable cabins nestled in misty grass across a pond. Someone who wasn't raised in a trailer park would call it charming. It did have a romantic vibe. I wrote it down.

Old Station cabins (sexy time)

I started sketching a woman's face…just because. I didn't realize until I finished it, but it was Kamilah's face. Her hair flowed out of my pen and onto the paper, wild and twisty. Exactly as it'd been when we'd kissed in the woods. I could see myself bringing her here…if I ever saw her again, proved to her I was good, and got her to fall in love with me. *If, if, if.*

I wasn't sharing a romantic moment with a beautiful lady though. I was sharing it with a grumpy, silent, middle-aged man. I spooned my bowl of instant oatmeal and tried not to ogle Hallenbeck's hearty breakfast—bacon, eggs, and pancakes from the country store—which he ate with surprising speed.

"The Korengal Valley. That was a bad one, right? You see some serious action?" I asked.

Hallenbeck's fork stopped in the air and he fixated on me. I hadn't realized it before, but there were flecks of amber—a ring of fire—in the dark brown of his irises. A chill raised the hair on my forearms.

"I mean, from the way you mentioned it…"

"Not that…kind of trip," he said.

I nodded, letting it go. There was a flickery ribbon in my chest waiting for the real Hallenbeck to stand up. A naïve wish echoing the tune of an Eminem song. *Will the real Hallenbeck please stand up? Please stand up, please stand up.*

We drove on to the next Cascade, Mount Eddy. We passed a National Park Service firefighter team dipping drip-torches on a hillside. My stomach twisted. I'd be there if not for Hallenbeck…

"Prescribed burn," I noted.

"Yup," Hallenbeck said, giving me some serious side-eye until I returned my focus to the road. *And I'd be out there if not for you and your inmate friend,* he said in my head.

I'm making up for that, I thought.

There was one deconsecrated church in the Mt. Eddy area. Half the roof was gone and the pews were scattered like bowling pins, with empty beer cans and used condoms strewn between them. The sky was a deep blue through the open roof. I imagined it gave a beautiful view of the starry night sky, and if you were raised religious, I guessed the wood-pecked Jesus on the cross watching over added to the thrill. The church structure was bristly with bird nests, but there were no signs of human construction. It was a teenage wasteland, not Wolfe's retirement project.

I convinced Hallenbeck to only stake out churches if there were signs of renovation or habitation. The relics of horny teenagers didn't count, so we moved on.

Next was Mount Shasta and its little sister Shastina. We sat at a Black Bear Diner in the town of Mt. Shasta. The grooved white and blue heights of the mountains were visible from our window seats. They rose into dark, knotted clouds that obscured the summits. Looked like rain.

I had a black coffee. Hallenbeck had biscuits and gravy, which I tried not to ogle once again. After we went over our church list and route plan, he went quiet. As usual.

"Lot of veterans in CalFire?" Was I a moron to bring this up? Probably. But I needed to break the ice.

"Eh. A lot more…in NPS."

"That wasn't for you?"

He nodded.

"You probably did well though. With that background."

"I did," he said. His narrowed eyes seared into me.

I shifted in my seat. *Mason, you* are *a moron.* I should say sorry, but he was being a dick. We were mission partners, traveling together and living under the same roof. He could stand to loosen up.

"At least…you're not thanking me for my service," he said.

"What's wrong with that?" I asked. At least he was talking.

"Superfish…superficial. Meaningless."

"Any other triggers I need to know about?"

"Triggers?" He chuffed. "That's…Zoomer bullshit."

I wasn't a shrink, but I was pretty sure that words or phrases that caused a negative reaction were the exact definition of a trigger.

"'Baby killers,'" Hallenbeck mused. "It's from…Vietnam, but still. Hate it."

"Glad you said something. I call people baby killers all the time."

"Yeah, yeah." He poked at his biscuits and another uncomfortable silence strained taut across the table.

"Those biscuits any good?" I asked.

"You can't…have any."

"Just trying to make conversation. Jesus."

"Not that kind of trip."

"Wouldn't it be good to have some, what do you call it, unit cohesion? Pretty sure that idea comes from the military. Pretty sure it's what you were trying to make happen with that hike and barbecue, my first day at La Cuenca." As soon as me, Ortiz, and the other FNGs had been shown our bunks, Hallenbeck had hiked Inmate Crew Nine up the tallest hill outside the camp and given us a speech about taking care of each other. He'd had plenty to say then.

"Did a lot…of hikes and barbecues back then. Lot less now," he muttered.

My bad hand screamed at me, and I unclenched my fists beneath the table. Just had to twist the knife, didn't he? The booth burped as I squirmed out and smacked the door to step outside. Huffing the bracing mountain air, I stared at the carved bear with its welcome sign.

I hated him, but I *couldn't* hate him. He was bitter and broken because of *me*. As much as he wasn't the man he used to be, I wasn't the man who'd done that to him. *Right?* This was my restitution. This would earn me a clean slate.

So get to work.

Trooping back inside, I flagged down our waitress and showed her Wolfe's picture. Our story was that his mother had terminal cancer and we needed to tell him since he was off the grid. The waitress hadn't seen him, but she called over the owner, a striking woman with gray hair and colorful tattoos.

"He looks familiar," she said. "He's that handyman, right? I think I've seen him at the Do It Best."

Poker face, Mason.

"What's that?"

"Hardware store."

Hallenbeck and I exchanged knowing looks. That fit Wolfe's retirement plan perfectly.

"Are there any abandoned churches around here?"

She told us about one that was up in the mountains, in fact. On the north side of Mt. Shasta near a town called McGreary. "'Bout a half-hour drive," she said helpfully.

It wasn't in my budget, but I gave her a $50 tip.

CHAPTER ELEVEN

Nick Curione

-1305-
-END-TO-END ENCRYPTION ACTIVE-

NC: They're looking for Wolfe.

EM: That's great news. Might find him for me and we can tie up that loose end. Put together a team. Funds have been deposited with a bonus applied for your insight.

NC: Thank you, sir.

EM: Stay on them and keep me posted.

NC: Of course, sir.

CHAPTER TWELVE

A drizzling rain pattered the windshield as we drove through the historic downtown of McGreary. Old West buildings and Old West-style facades dominated the town's main street. Collector cars lined the curbs and there were five antique stores in two blocks. A Crows Point Saloon had those swinging double doors from every Western ever in front of a regular modern one. It was picturesque and absorbed with the past. Peaceful. Way more peaceful than Wolfe deserved.

Online maps took us to five different churches in McGreary and none of them were abandoned. The priest at one, St. Michael's, gave us directions to a church that wasn't on the internet. Up in the mountains, like the diner owner had been talking about. I wove through a maze of potholed, cracked roads as the rain intensified. The pines pressed closer and closer until branches began skittering on the panels.

The road came to a gate that was chained closed. *PRIVATE PROPERTY. NO TRESSPASSING.* The gate was part of a fence stretching into the forest on both sides. Past it and down that forest road, there was supposed to be an abandoned church, the one that might hold our quarry. Hallenbeck set his hunting rifle on the shag carpet divider between our seats.

I stopped the vehicle and gave him my full attention. He returned it.

"No more beating around the bush," I said. It was time for Bad Cop. "We're a team, and I need to know what you can and can't do, or we don't go any farther."

His jaw tightened. He regarded me in silence for a moment.

"When do you need your cane? When don't you? Can you hold onto that rifle?"

"You're right," he sighed. "I...won't," he laughed abruptly, "won't give you...the laundry list...of medical jargon. But I'll explain." He took a deep breath. "You know how I talk. That I...have some spasticity. That shit...turns me into the Tin Man without...his oil."

He pulled up the fly of his jeans—*shff*—it was a Velcro tab instead of a zipper.

"Got issues...with fine motor control. I may not be the marksman I used to be...but I can handle a weapon. My balance is okay. Not...great. Okay. Hills, uneven surfaces...can be tough. And it hurts."

"Walking?"

"Everything. Abnormal growth in...my hips and shoulders.

Gets worse…by the end of the day, or just…activity." He tapped his cane. "So this helps."

The T in TBI was no joke. It had exacted terrible changes on his body. Mentally, maybe it was the reason he was so different than the man I'd known before the injury. I wanted to say I was sorry, but now that he was finally leveling with me, I knew sympathy would only hurt right now. Instead, I said, "We're gonna find him."

He nodded.

"Oh, and…insomnia."

"I noticed." Half the time I got up to take my 2 am piss, he was reading a book by the light of his phone.

"Thanks," I said. "I'm trusting that if you say you can handle this, you can. So. Are you up for this?"

In answer, Hallenbeck slung his hunting rifle on his shoulder, put his cane under his other arm, and got out. He went back down the road, looking around, then waved me over. I backed up and drove off-road through the gap in the trees he'd found. I waited as he studied our improvised off-ramp, making sure we hadn't left any signs. He gave a thumbs-up and caned his way ahead to be the pathfinder. I followed him, the motorhome lurching and rattling over the uneven ground. The tires snapped branches, squelched mud, and rustled undergrowth. My shoulders tensed and I tried not to think about the fact that I only had one spare and no AAA. Hallenbeck waved to stop—we'd reached the fence.

I grabbed my bag of tricks n' treats and climbed out. The cool and wet wrapped me up like a blanket. Wood posts stood every 20 feet or so, droplets pinging down the barbed wire threads strung between them.

I dug in my bag for gloves. Better not to cut it and leave signs someone came through. "If I pull the wire up, can you get under it?" I asked. He'd probably done this kind of thing in Marine training, but he wasn't that spry young soldier anymore.

With an actual smile on his face, Hallenbeck used his cane handle to pull the wire up.

"Nice," I said. Crawling under, pine needles scratched my arms and dirt clung to my clothes. Better than a barb tearing into my back. I took the cane and did the same for him. Straining to hold the wire as high as possible, I could only watch as he went through, stiff and grunting. He allowed me to help him up though.

"You all right?"

He winced and leaned hard on his cane. Then sighed and held out his rifle.

"You…take point."

I took it without hesitation, which he clocked with a squint. No skin off my back—I didn't want him shooting anybody. And while I wasn't gonna shoot anyone either, it was a useful threat. Especially if Wolfy really was here.

I took a stun gun out of my bag and he accepted it without comment. Socking the rifle butt in my shoulder and keeping the muzzle low, I went forward.

Rain dribbling down our faces, we tramped through slippery needles, fallen branches, and rot, following the road from within the forest. The trees opened to a clearing green with grass and gray with mist.

A church rose out of the gray on a knotted hill, its earthtone belltower piercing the mist. Paint bubbled away at the edges, revealing brick, wood, and concrete. Rainwater rivulets split and merged on a rose window pocked with missing panes. There were no vehicles in its cracked parking lot.

I paused. We listened. Rain drummed shingles and spattered the empty lot. Winds gusted, and there was an unidentified *whap-whap-whap*. Hallenbeck nodded and we circled around to the other side of the hill. The whapping sound was a blue tarp flailing over a hole in the roof, its fastener broken.

I arched an eyebrow at Hallenbeck. He nodded. The tarp was a promising sign. Atop the hill, at the corner of the building, an outdoor tent stood surrounded by tools, lumber, and construction supplies. Even more promising. We trudged up the slippery, snarled hill.

"Cover me," Hallenbeck said.

I stopped and pointed the rifle at the tent. He unzipped it and threw open the flap. A sleeping bag, flashlight, used water bottles. An oniony smell filled my nostrils, almost overpowering. Sweat.

"Clear," Hallenbeck said.

"Church?"

"Yeah," he replied.

The building had the standard t-shaped footprint. Crucifix-shaped is what they were going for, but to me it looked like a stubby "t." The main entrance—narthex—lay opposite us at the bottom of the t. We were at the top corner, and the back door facing us was padlocked shut. A thrill raced up my spine. *This has to be it.*

"Can your…locksmith tool open that padlock?" Hallenbeck asked.

"It could. But let's take the windows." I pointed my chin at a missing windowpane in the south-facing transept: a stumpy arm of the t. I slung the rifle and clambered through, and Hallenbeck grumbled as I helped him through.

A metal gong boomed off the walls. I snapped the rifle into my hands and crouched, angling it over the dusky interior. Nothing else made a sound, nothing else moved.

Hallenbeck cleared his throat and pointed at the floor—a rolling pipe came to a stop. He'd stumbled on it. The transept was filled with a web of disconnected, discarded pipes. I got out front and wove through into the cross of the t, where a rotted altar met the pew-lined nave.

Burgundy carpet squelched at my feet. A musty funk tickled my nose, and there was a hint of sawdust in it. Smothered by rain clouds, the stained glass that remained presented the space in suffocated kaleidoscope. A dotted line of water drained from the ceiling into a rotted hole, making concentric rings of decay. Through carpet, through pad, through wood, through cement. With time, water was as corrosive as the Facehugger's acid blood. The big, open, one-story stretch of the church was empty.

I climbed creaking steps into the belltower. A six-foot-tall bronze bell was lodged in the wood floor, but otherwise, the tower was empty. I went back down to the nave and Hallenbeck motioned me over, pointing at details emerging in the sickly light. The confessional was built from new lumber. It had sawdust on the floor around it—and a cot. A break area?

I hustled down the nave to the narthex, an entrance chamber walled off from the pews and the altar. Stacks of lumber, more sawdust, and a lumpy tarp. I ripped it away. A table saw, workbench, and power tools. The stench of man-sweat steeped the area. Hallenbeck caned in, eyes wide.

"Do you think?" I asked.

"Maybe. No smoke…no smoking gun." The corners of his mouth tugged up, then got back in line. Stifling his excitement.

It fit his recollection perfectly. A town in the foothills of a Cascade Mountain. Spending "retirement" rebuilding an abandoned church. But he was right. We had to be sure.

We combed the place, fleecing out empty Red Bulls, broken drill bits, and a pyrography pen. I'd used one in shop class—it was good for soldering, leather cutting, or woodburning art. We didn't find any personal identifying information.

Venturing back into the rain, we splashed over to the tent and rifled through it. Toothbrush and toothpaste, beard trimmer, towels and rags and a waterproof container the size of a dictionary with what looked like a dictionary inside. No CalFire patches or hats. Wolfe wasn't stupid.

…if this place was even his. It *had* to be though.

While Hallenbeck pawed every stitch of the sleeping bag, I clicked open the container. The big tome within was a hardcover Catholic Bible. I flipped through it, hoping for a secret compartment cut out of the pages. But it was just a book. When I closed it shut, something clinked. I pulled out the noisy object from the bottom of the container. A dog collar.

"Did Wolfe have a dog?" I asked.

"Shit… Yeah. Big black lab or something. Goofy thing. Shit… What was its name?"

Fogged from the moisture, I wiped the tag to read the name

engraved there.

"Snickers?"

Hallenbeck looked over sharply.

"Yeah." He knelt next to me, no longer stifling his excitement, and took the collar in his hands. "Snickers."

"How's that for a smoking gun?"

Hallenbeck grinned.

CHAPTER THIRTEEN

The rain slackened to a drizzle after nightfall, and fog closed in around the church like a pewter cocoon. The narthex was dry but a draft knifed through the church, cutting to the bone. Hallenbeck dozed against the tarp-covered workbench. It was hour six of our stakeout.

During the first hour, we'd swapped stories about Wolfe. The Sean he'd worked with at La Cuenca Conservation Camp had been a "hard worker. Kind of shy. Went out for drinks occasion… occasionally. One time, he really went off…about the pay. Guess… he had money problems." I recalled the second time Wolfe had tried to kill me (with rattlesnakes), but I'd survived and pinned him on the forest floor. Holding a rock over his head, I'd demanded some answers. He broke immediately—pleading and pathetic. I'd smashed his knee with the rock to take him out of the game.

Apparently it worked, because he was reported missing shortly after.

"So he…responds to physical threats," Hallenbeck had said.

"Let's try other methods first. We gotta convince him to tell the police what he knows."

"But we need to know…what that is first. Is he under Marshall's…protection? Is he on his own?"

"Yeah." We did need to confirm that Wolfe had something *usable*. But I was also remembering when I'd confronted Grayson Graham to get a recording that confirmed his acts of arson. LA Sherriff's Department Deputy Richard Martin had been very clear that the statement couldn't be coerced or obtained under duress. "And I'm saying that bringing the police a roughed-up fugitive who we claim is ready to confess isn't a good look."

"I'm…tracking." All the same, Hallenbeck had taken a hammer from Wolfe's toolbox and tucked it through his belt. Now, its handle ticked against the wood floor in the rhythm of his stuttering breaths as he slept. Avoiding coercion and duress was legit, but more than anything, I thought of what Kamilah had said. Being a good man was "a choice you have to make day-in and day-out." Someday, when this was all over, I could tell her I'd done things right. Maybe it would be enough to win her over. *Maybe maybe maybe.*

My mind had drifted to how weird it was that a man who'd tried to kill me had adored a goofy lab named Snickers when my phone dinged. The motion sensor I'd planted at the gate had been tripped. A rusty pickup truck rattled up the road. As it turned into the lot, I saw the bearded face and deep-set eyes behind the wheel. The beard was new and the face under it was thinner, but it was Wolfe.

I tapped Hallenbeck awake. He leaned his cane against the wall and crouched behind the lumber stack with his rifle. I picked up a stun gun and slipped out a window. I stalked below the summit of the hill to circle around and get to the rear of the truck, crossing Wolfe's path without detection as he limped to the front door. *I gave him that limp*, I thought with a thrill.

Clunk. The magnet of the GPS tracker fastened to the inside of the rear bumper. I jostled it and it didn't budge—strong hold.

I crept behind him, the drizzle blanketing the sounds of movement. *This time, I'm setting the trap.* Wolfe unlocked the front door and entered the narthex. I slipped in behind him as Hallenbeck stood up and pointed the rifle at Wolfe's chest.

Stay off the trigger, I thought, and squeezed my own. Silver flashed. *Tk-tk-tk-tk!* Gasping, Wolfe toppled onto his face with two wires in his back. Twitching and cursing, he crawled onto his side and looked up.

"Mason Jones," he wheezed.

Hallenbeck set a work light next to Wolfe's face and flicked it on. "And…Mark," he said, as Wolfe squeezed his eyes shut, reaching out.

"Don't…move," he added.

Wolfe stopped moving. Strange, sickle-shaped scars on his face glistened in the blinding light. He blinked rapidly, glassy eyes racing around the room. There was nothing in reach, and we'd removed every sharp tool and blunt object—what Hallenbeck called weapons of opportunity. Damn but it felt good to get the jump on *him* this time.

My own eyes watering from the light, I yanked his hands

behind his back and zip-tied his wrists. His cheeks were hollow. His forearms like cords. He'd always been wiry, and he was down to the last wires now.

Good. Living in squalor, wasting away in a ruin? *This* was the retirement Wolfe deserved.

"Gonna pat you down," I said. "The barbs are still in and Mark's gun is loaded."

"Mason," he said.

"Shut up."

I frisked him. Raised, squarish welts dappled his arms, and when I checked his boots for knives, they protruded from his ankles too. They were brands.

"What happened to you?" I asked.

"Focus…Mason," Hallenbeck said.

"I'm focused." *Dad*, I stopped myself from saying. I pulled up Wolfe's shirt—no weapons in his waistband. More squarish brands across stomach and sides, going up to his jutting ribs. Finishing, I held out the results of my search to Hallenbeck. A Leatherman, his keys, and a grimy K-95 mask.

"Not as good as your last one," I said, gesturing with his Leatherman.

"Corner," Hallenbeck said. "Sit."

Wolfe lurched and sat on the lumber stack. The halogen beam irradiated rings of the geometric welts spangled across his biceps and forearms. Add the black t-shirt and jeans and his darting eyes, and he looked like a demented rock star.

"We're here to talk about Erik Marshall and Grayson Graham," I said.

It was hard to tell in the halogen's glare, but he seemed to pale. His voice dropped to a whisper. "Who sent you?"

"We're not…answering questions. We're…asking them."

Wolfe smirked. "Or what?"

Hallenbeck slung his rifle and took out the hammer. He used it to point at Wolfe's knees.

"Which…is the good one?"

"You wouldn't."

"Been off the grid for a minute, haven't you?" I remarked. "Haven't met the new and improved Mark Hallenbeck."

Wolfe shifted, squaring his shoulders. An awkward and probably painful movement with his arms tied behind him.

"I have money," he said. "I can give you…80, no, 90 thousand. 90 thousand dollars."

"Yeah, really looks like you're rolling in the dough."

"I was well paid. Filthy lucre," he spat. "I was…" He sighed and left the thought unfinished. "Now, I only use money for materials and tools. If you leave me in peace, it's all yours."

"We're not like you. We don't take payoffs."

Wolfe's eyes fell to the floor. He was quiet and still, and I held a finger up, signaling Hallenbeck. *Give him a moment to stew.*

Wolfe's neck corded, and the veins on his arms bulged. He was straining to break the zip ties. Failing, he shouted in frustration.

"What can I do to get you to leave me in peace?"

Hallenbeck and I exchanged a look. There was nothing. We needed him to come with us and tell his tales to the authorities.

"To enjoy…your retirement?" Hallenbeck asked, fixing Wolfe with the harsh glare he'd used on me in his study.

"This isn't retirement," Wolfe said.

"Then…then what is it?"

"That's between me and God."

"You and God?" I burst, my pulse thundering in my ears.

Hallenbeck marched on Wolfe with the hammer raised.

"Whoa." I held him back. Wolfe hunched and brought a knee up defensively, but he didn't cower. Hallenbeck's eyes were lethal, and I couldn't tell if it was an act or not. At least we'd established Good Cop/Bad Cop roles, although…my Good Cop approach hadn't even worked when I'd needed Hallenbeck to level about his TBI. And he was my teammate.

Think, Mason. I couldn't relate to the God part, but Wolfe did seem to have regrets, and that I could relate to. Maybe Ash River weighed on him, like it did me. What would make *me* talk?

"Just between you and God?" I asked, thinking of the Patchwork's official death toll. "Twenty-nine people died."

"And I've accounted for them." He rolled his shoulder to point at the scars on his face. "That's what these are. One for every life lost."

He'd cut himself 29 times. Having been stabbed and slashed by my enemies, I couldn't imagine the madness it took to do that to yourself…again and again and again. Had he started on his face, or ended there? A chill trickled up my spine and I eyed Hallenbeck.

The old Marine had a grim smile on his face.

At least he isn't beating him with the hammer.

"The homes too," Wolfe whispered. He twisted to show the brands on his arms. With his wrists bound behind him, it was like a backward version of a body builder pose.

I looked closer at the brands. They were house shapes. Not outlines, but solid—completely filled in. And each one was slightly different. Not made with the same brand. Each one custom, seared into the skin individually. *The pyrography pen.*

"You burned these into yourself?"

"Each one is a hundred homes. Not enough skin," he cackled.

I did some quick math—15,217 homes were lost to the Patchwork fire complex, and each brand represented a hundred homes. He'd branded himself 152 times—but only because he didn't have enough skin to do it 15,000 times. I choked down a surge of pre-vomit saliva filling my mouth.

Wolfe gestured to himself, and the church in progress.

"That's what this is. Penance. And you're standing between me and my salvation."

"What about the penance you owe him?" I indicated Hallenbeck. "*You're* the reason Graham got on the fireline in the first place."

"You're right," he said, eyes down. He was silent for a moment. He twisted again, showing off a blank part of his skin canvas. "There's room for you, Mark. What symbol should it be?" He looked around, but we'd taken all his tools into the nave. "Where'd you put the burner? You can do it yourself." His eyes gleamed. He wanted Hallenbeck to brand him.

Ice cold, Hallenbeck shot me a look, like, *Why not?*

It was sickening. But…maybe if we "scratched his back" like the masochist wanted, he'd scratch ours and tell us something useful about Marshall. A good trade, right?

Wrong.

"We're not gonna brand you," *whack job*, I stopped myself from saying. I wanted to ply the psycho with honey, not vinegar. "Why don't you keep the skin you have left and tell us what you know about Marshall?"

"I owe penance for my sins. I don't owe you information."

"So you're still protecting Marshall."

"*No*," Wolfe growled.

"He really knows how to pick 'em," I replied, playing off his anger at being lumped in with Marshall. "Still has your loyalty. Here you are, cornered, alone, completely at our mercy, and you're still his man."

"I'm not his man!" he shouted.

"Then how are you still alive?"

Wolfe shook his head and looked away.

He's hiding something.

"No…choice then," Hallenbeck growled, advancing with the hammer again. I stopped him again. We weren't getting anywhere.

"Let him stew," I whispered. My face was hot and my muscles twitchy. I took deep breaths to stay in control.

Grumbling, Hallenbeck backed off.

I tied Wolfe's hands to a stud so he couldn't slip them under his feet. Leaving the doors from the narthex to the nave open, Hallenbeck and I shuffled into a pew. He set the hammer down and massaged his fingers.

"That was just for show, right?"

He didn't answer.

I left him and went to a stained-glass window. The lead sky made the colors murky. I'd just been starting to trust Hallenbeck again.

Not enough skin.

A sour taste lingered in my mouth. It wasn't just Hallenbeck, and it wasn't just that we weren't getting anywhere with Wolfe. When the stakeout had begun, all I could think about was how this man had had the life I'd been refused and, as Hallenbeck would say, pissed on it. Now, all I could think about was his cackle.

Not enough skin.

I shivered.

CHAPTER FOURTEEN

I couldn't get it out of my head. Unsettled, I took out my phone to call Ortiz. I needed a Catholic to weigh in on what Wolfe had done to himself.

"You calling…the police?" Hallenbeck asked.

"No. Not yet."

"Agreed." Hallenbeck looked at me with respect. It felt good.

At this point, I think a normal person *would* call the cops. We'd located a fugitive who was an accomplice to the most destructive acts of arson in California history. But he wasn't talking. *Not enough skin.*

"Yo!" Ortiz answered. "Guess what?"

"What?"

"The baby kicked!"

Baby? I'd almost forgotten Ortiz had another kid on the way.

What a shitty friend I was.

"That's awesome!" I said, and I meant it. Now that I had my own good news to share, I could manage to be genuinely happy for him. *Shitty, shitty friend.*

"I was on the couch next to her when it happened. I cried, yo. The first kick! I wasn't there when this stuff was happening with Emily."

"Congrats, man. That's really cool."

"Thanks, bro. What's up?"

"We found him." I grinned.

"Fuck yeah. Get anything from him?"

"Not yet. He's being a little bitch."

While I told Ortiz about the exchange with Wolfe, I went outside and circled around the church, sheltering from the rain under the eaves.

"Is that what you guys believe?" I asked.

"Naw, man." Ortiz sounded offended. "He's crazy. All you gotta do is ask God for forgiveness."

"That's it?"

"Yeah," Ortiz said. "I mean, you gotta confess to a priest, be legit contrite and shit, but yeah, that's basically it. Wolfe could be forgiven."

"That's convenient."

Ortiz *humphed* but said nothing, disagreeing but not wanting to press it.

I wished he was here. Even contemplated asking him to join the interrogation…but that'd be selfish. His family needed him more than I did.

"Give Emily a squeeze and tell your parole officer I'm up to no good. She'll love that."

Ortiz laughed. "Stay safe, *hermano*."

I told him I would.

It didn't make me feel any better about Wolfe's cackle. I didn't even know why it disturbed me so much. *Not enough skin.*

With midnight approaching, Hallenbeck and I resolved to make another go at Wolfe in the morning. But first, our prisoner needed to piss. I cut the ties to the stud and motioned to his plastic camp toilet, which we'd found and brought in from under the eaves.

"That's only for number two," he said. "I go to the tree line to piss."

"We can empty it," I said.

"I need to stretch my legs."

"Bend and touch your toes."

"With walking. Of all people, don't *you* want to treat prisoners humanely?"

Asshole had me there. I nodded and picked up my stun gun.

"Don't try anything."

Hallenbeck picked up his rifle and Wolfe rolled his eyes. We led him in front of us out to the tree line. It was misty with spritzing rain. I motioned to Hallenbeck, who raised his rifle in warning, and then I snipped the zip ties from his wrists.

Grimacing, Wolfe unzipped. I looked away, but Hallenbeck kept his eyes on his back. Someone had to. There was no sound of liquid splashing on the ground.

"Might take a minute. I'm a very private person," he grunted.

Finally, I heard the stream of liquid spattering. I fought an urge to throw him down into his own piss; I'd been pissing in the woods when he'd pulled me down into a ravine and sicced rattlesnakes on me.

When he was done, I zip-tied his wrists back together, and his scars and brands gave me another bout of pre-vomit nausea. I spat into the mist. As we walked back to the church, I thought of how he'd reacted to me calling him Marshall's man and had an idea.

"Sean," I said, and he seemed startled to hear his first name, "all these...marks. You did this to yourself because you know you did wrong. Because you did what Erik Marshall told you to do."

"Where are...his scars?" Hallenbeck asked, catching on. "When will...when will *he* be punished?"

"He'll face his own judgment," Wolfe whispered, eyes flicking at the cross over the door.

"In the afterlife?" I scoffed as we went inside. "What about the people he hurts next? As long as he's free, he won't stop. It'll only get worse." The more you get away with something, the bolder you get. I had.

"I'll pray for them."

"Jesus Christ," I said.

"Hey," Wolfe warned, rolling his shoulders to indicate our surroundings. Ortiz was snippy about that stuff too. Something about the Lord's name. I closed my eyes so Wolfe wouldn't see them rolling. *Honey, not vinegar.*

"Guess we'll...call the police then," Hallenbeck said. I'd wanted to let Wolfe stew before trying this tactic, but it was out of the bag now. "Render...you unto Caesar. Wonder what'll happen in lock up?"

Marshall would have him Epsteined within a day, of course.

Wolfe shrugged. "It is not in a man to determine his steps," he said.

That sounded biblical. And again, it made me think he was hiding something. What did he have up his sleeve?

"You'll cut yourself for what you've done wrong, but you won't lift a finger to prevent it," I summarized. "What does your Bible say about that?"

"I can't stop Marshall. *You* can't stop Marshall. There are no lines he won't cross."

Once again, we weren't getting anywhere. I thought I'd be able to reach him, but I wasn't even close. I caught Hallenbeck's eyes and he nodded. Time to call it a night.

I tied Wolfe's hands to the stud again. And, because I was trying to do the good-guy thing, I uncapped a bottle of water and set it on the lumber next to him. It'd be awkward, but he'd be able to bend and grab it with his mouth.

"Cheers."

Hallenbeck paused, studying his old coworker.

"Why did you...become a firefighter?"

Wolfe hung his head.

"To...protect people?"

He looked back up, his eyes red and wet. Those eyes said *yes*.

Hallenbeck walked away, shooting me a significant look: *Let him chew on that*. I nodded. Hallenbeck laid his sleeping mat down in a dry spot of the nave, while I stayed in the narthex and settled down a few yards from a man who'd tried to kill me twice. I didn't know if it was the stun gun at my side, the knife on my calf, or the way the man hunched like a broke-neck crow in the harsh glow of the work light. Whatever it was, I slept fine.

Until I didn't. The old man stood over a barrel fire in his turnout gear. He took a cattle brand out of the flames. The glowing, H-shaped iron cast heatwaves that magnified his bitter eyes. Wolfe, a flickering scarecrow, watched with wide, gleeful eyes, but it was Hallenbeck who said, "*Not enough skin,*" as he pressed the brand into my bare chest.

"Mason."

I bolted awake. Wolfe was calling my name. My pulse thundered in my ears and the wood beneath me was damp with sweat.

"Mason," he said again.

Back twinging, I sat up and looked at him. He remained bound, but he was sitting up straight now. His eyes clearer and gaze steadier. I checked the time. 3:36. Smack dab in the middle of the witching hour. Which made sense, because the man across from me looked like a creature cursed.

"I want to show you something," he said.

My juvenile, sleep-fogged mind thought: *Better not be your dick.* The smart portion of my brain won the day and I realized he meant something important.

"Is it about Marshall?"

"Yes," he said.

"Where?" I cut the ties to the stud but left the zip ties around his wrists.

I eyed Hallenbeck, who was still asleep in the nave. Good for him—no insomnia tonight. Wolfe shook his head.

"Not Mark." He couldn't even look at him. Something he couldn't show the firefighter, but could show the criminal. What the old Marine had said had really reached him. I decided not to wake him.

Wolfe led me to the belltower. Me and Wolfe were enemies, but there was a strange kinship chaining us together. An intimacy among sinners. I let him trudge ahead of me up the groaning stairs, my stun gun ready.

From the tower, the edge of the forest was now visible. The cocoon of fog had retreated and the rain had stopped. The air was cold and still.

Wolfe pointed to the six-foot-tall bell on the floor with a foot.

"I'm gonna need my hands."

I frisked him again—just in case—and he was still clean. I cut the ties from his wrists.

"We need to lift this up," he said.

"Go for it," I said, backing up so I was out of reach.

"Can you help?"

"No." I wasn't about to put myself in a vulnerable position.

"Okay, I'm using this as a lever," Wolfe warned me, picking up a plank. Grunting, he lifted the bronze monstrosity up just enough to stick the plank under the lip. He shoved it in farther and began levering the bell up from the floor.

Crack. The damp plank snapped and the bell *whunked* back onto the floor.

He gave me a scornful look.

"Fine," I said, and hunched down on one side of the bell. It was a strain just to get the lip in my hands. Beads of water dribbled down the bronze curve and pooled in my palms. "One, two, three, lift." Quads trembling, hands crushing from the weight, we lifted the bell up and toppled it on its side.

Bong! I hoped that didn't wake Hallenbeck.

There, where the bell had been, was a thick black safe. It looked about 2 feet wide, 2 feet deep, and 3 feet tall. It was also bolted to the floor. Wolfe caught his breath and leaned against the stone windowsill.

"Thanks," he said.

"Hands where I can see them," I breathed.

He laid his hands on his hips, palms up.

"What is this?" I asked, motioning to the safe.

"The only thing keeping me alive if he finds me. Evidence."

"Prove it," I said, heart thudding in my chest. I didn't reveal an ounce of the excitement I felt.

"Tell me how this stops him. Tell me how this is different from last time," Wolfe said.

"I can't do that without seeing what you have. You'll have to trust me."

Wolfe smiled ruefully. "I'm a penitent, not an idiot."

"And I gave you a bad knee instead of killing you."

I thought he'd huff and puff, but he hung his head and dug a fingernail into a brand on his arm. "I deserve worse."

"Not gonna get an argument from me on that. Just open the goddamn safe."

He frowned at that, but he knelt down in front of it.

"I always imagined sharing it one day. When my penance was done."

"And when would that be?"

Wolfe just spun the tumbler.

Clunk.

I expected a space that size to be filled up, but of the three shelves within, only the middle one had anything on it. Draped in shadows sat two sandwich-sized hard drives, an accordion folder, and three stacks of cash.

Wolfe handed me a sheet of paper from the folder. It was a bank statement showing a $10,000 deposit into the account of a…

"David Marlowe?" I asked aloud.

"My alias for the Deutsche Bank account Marshall put my payments in. This is one of those deposits."

I squinted at the paper in the dim light.

"The deposit is from 'Hearthside,' whatever that is," I said.

"That's a nonprofit of Marshall's. I checked."

Holy shit. I was so amazed it made me dizzy.

"If the rest of that is like *this*, we're in business."

"It is," Wolfe said. "The hard drives have all the original versions, plus emails and texts about…" he couldn't meet my eyes, "what he told me to do."

About the orders to kill me. I couldn't even be upset about it—this evidence was a slam dunk. I almost wanted to hug the crazy bastard, so I distracted myself with logistics to avoid it.

"How the hell'd you get that up here?" I motioned at the safe.

"Chain hoist."

"Electric?"

"Hand."

"Damn." Good workout. Definitely a big addition to the sweat infusion of his tent. I ushered him back down to the narthex, zip-tied his wrists, and gave him a blanket. "I'll see you in the morning," I said.

"And then?"

"I'll have a plan."

I didn't know much about the right thing, but Wolfe was doing it. Unable to believe what *I* was doing, I extended my hand.

Wolfe was just as stunned. He shook it.

"Thank you," I said.

CHAPTER FIFTEEN

The pre-dawn sky was ultraviolet with a glimmer of orange on the horizon. The meager light didn't penetrate the stained glass, and honestly, I was glad that Hallenbeck's face was indistinct in the gloom of the church. He was pissed.

"Don't si...sideline me again," he huffed.

"That was the only way it was gonna happen. Outlaw to outlaw. That's what you wanted from me, right?" I smirked, watching Wolfe through the open doors of the narthex. He was eating some oatmeal I'd given him. With his wrists tied together, it looked like some kind of gastronomic prayer ritual. An awkward one. *Maybe he's earned some time off the cuffs.*

"Cocky bastard. He could've...thrown you off the belltower."

"Aw, shucks. I didn't know you cared."

"It was stupid."

"I may be the one he showed it to, but *you're* the reason he wanted to." The man deserved some kudos. "Nice work."

Hallenbeck smiled—briefly—then tapped his cane emphatically. "Time for…next steps."

I agreed and got out my phone to dial Sizzlean. At least, that was his name in my phone.

"It's five in the morning," LASD Deputy Richard Martin answered, groaning.

"Sorry. I got something big for you."

"For me? Or are you asking for help?" His tone was as harsh as battery acid.

"It's both. What the hell, man?" I'd taken bullets for this guy.

A sigh rasped from the speaker. "Are you safe?"

"Yeah. Look, I found Sean Wolfe."

A long silence stretched. I checked to make sure the call hadn't dropped. It hadn't. *This is a big fucking deal!*

"From the Erik Marshall case!" I added.

"I'm going to stop you right there, Mason. I can't handle another crisis, all right? I've got my own problems."

I couldn't think of a problem that outweighed *this*. What the hell was going on?

"Are *you* safe?" I asked.

"I crossed swords with a gang," he said. "This one has badges."

"Shit. Is Kamilah safe?" A knot pulled tight in my chest.

"She is." The knot unwound. "And I'm working to keep it that way."

Mind racing, I forced myself to focus on the matter at hand. Wolfe. The safe. Bringing down Marshall.

"And for your sake, drop whatever you've got on Marshall. He's made of Teflon. Nothing sticks."

Richard hung up.

Tensing up, I sat down hard in a pew. Richard was the only cop I trusted. I'd been banking on his help. Wolfe and the safe of evidence needed to go to law enforcement through someone who could vouch for me. Thanks to a rap sheet full of awful mistakes, they might think I was involved with Wolfe and Marshall. Hallenbeck could vouch for me, but with my past it was more likely they'd make him into an accomplice.

"That bad?" Hallenbeck asked.

I nodded. Who else could I go to? My old lawyer, Davit? But there was no money in it, so he wouldn't help.

"Do you know any cops you trust?" I asked.

"With information that…incriminates Erik Marshall? Hell no."

"Shit."

That left me with only one other option. I wasn't sure if I could trust her, but I dialed the contact known as Agent Speedcore in my phone.

Jasmine Boone answered on the second ring.

"Jonesy! How's my favorite absconsion risk?"

"I'm not sure if you're the right person for this, like, jurisdiction-wise, but I don't know who else to go to. I have something—I mean—*if* I had information about criminal activity and a wanted fugitive, would you be able to help?"

"Slow down, Mason. Tell me what's going on."

She'd called me by my actual *name.*

"I'd rather tell you in person." It was paranoid, but it would keep the information out of the law enforcement grapevine longer. Which kept it away from Marshall longer.

"Okay. Where are you?"

"And it might be dangerous."

"I understand. Where are you?"

"Near Mt. Shasta." I texted her a navigation pin.

"Six hundred miles." She whistled, overwhelming the microphone so it blasted static. "Gonna take at least eight hours then. Hey, I get to use my siren!"

"Does that mean you're gonna help?" I drove my knuckles into my thighs.

"Mason, I'm a sworn peace officer. Of course I'm going to help."

I laid down in the pew, muscles melting in relief.

You trust her?" Wolfe asked. We sat in the sun outside his tent. He rubbed his wrists, now free, against his jeans. I had Hallenbeck's rifle slung over my shoulder.

"I do," I said. *We have to,* I thought, and exchanged a glance with Hallenbeck. He'd driven the motorhome out of the forest— without crashing, I was happy to see— and parked it at the back of the church. The microwave beeped and he caned into the kitchen. He usually didn't need it in the morning, but yesterday had been a very active day.

"You think she can get me into witness protection?"

"I think cooperation is the best option, yeah." I didn't know what he would qualify for, and was even less sure what he deserved.

Wolfe sighed and studied his church.

"What if you just took the evidence?"

I stopped myself from groaning in exasperation. We needed him *and* the evidence.

"No more…hiding. No…running. That's done," Hallenbeck barked, stomping out of the motorhome with a paper plate of sausages, bacon, and some eggs. My mouth watered—not that Hallenbeck would give any to me.

"What about my church?"

It was a good question. Wolfe had explained that he owned the land under another alias. Whatever deal he got for his long overdue evidence and testimony, I had no idea if he'd get to keep the land or if the government would repossess it. Add the variables of sentencing, and protective custody or witness protection, and he might never even see the place again.

"I don't know," I said.

"It wasn't supposed to be like this." Wolfe's entire body sagged. It reminded me of a Quikcrete bag hitting asphalt.

"Are you…fucking kidding?" Hallenbeck snapped.

I made a surreptitious *bring it down a notch* motion at him. *Be nice.* We needed Wolfe calm and cooperative.

"That for all of us?" Wolfe changed the subject, motioning at Hallenbeck's breakfast.

I chuckled and shook my head. *That's not how Hallenbeck rolls.*

"It's for me and Mason," he said, and separated a second paper plate from the first, giving me a plastic fork and a heap of steaming protein. A corner of his mouth twitched up.

I couldn't help but sit a little straighter as I took it. *I guess*

I'd earned that. Wolfe nodded, an *It's what I deserve* look on his face. I inhaled everything except for a smidge of scrambled egg before realizing I had meant to give some to him. The yellow curd glistened in the sun. It'd be an insult to give *that* to him, and…I *had* already fed him this morning. I hoovered that up too.

Hallenbeck had that old glint in his eyes as he tossed the empty plates in our trash bag. I didn't know what to make of it, but I hoped he kept it up. I unlocked the road gate, checked the motion sensor planted there, and we waited for Boone's arrival.

It was almost 2 pm when her car pulled into the church lot. The sun had driven us inside and the stained-glass kaleidoscope of color in the nave was bright and cheery. We went out into the heat to meet her. My throat was thick as she stepped out in her black polo and khakis, a gun on her hip and a smile on her lips. She interrupted my babble of thanks and marched up to Wolfe, who stood anxiously to the side.

"What's your name?"

"Sean Cillian Wolfe."

"Thank you," she said, and took out handcuffs. "You're under arrest for conspiracy and attempted murder. You have the right to remain silent. Anything you say can and will be used against you in a court of law. You have a right to an attorney…" She went on with his Miranda rights while cuffing him.

Wolfe accepted this without comment, but his wide eyes kept flicking at me.

"He's cooperating," I reminded her. "He's handing over evidence."

"Understood. That doesn't erase the warrant out for him."

When Wolfe was officially arrested, she came over to me and whispered, "It's going to be okay. I have to do things the right way here."

I nodded. Wolfe and I had talked about this earlier, when I took him to unlock the road gate for her arrival, but now that it was happening I couldn't tamp the ache in my gut. And I wasn't even the one in bracelets.

She took us each into the confessional separately for individual interviews. Wolfe first, then Hallenbeck, then me. I touched the smooth, unfinished wood of the confessional. Straight lines. Sturdy joints. Comfortable seat. The cracked penitent had done a good job. The mesh thing I'd seen in movies hadn't been put in yet, so I had a clear view of Boone's framed, shadowed face in the adjoining booth. She was the priest in this scenario, and I told her everything. I hoped Hallenbeck and Wolfe had done the same.

Boone nodded and made some notes in her phone. She had that same meditative look I'd seen when she'd been reviewing my resume—and she'd actually been thinking about some guy.

"So what happened with that dude who was into you?" It wasn't the best time for this conversation, but I couldn't help it. I was still carrying a torch for Kamilah and I was curious about the dude that carried one for her.

Boone laughed. "I called him up on the way, actually. He's based in NorCal."

"He the one you mentioned on the phone?"

"Yup!"

While coordinating things on the call this morning, Boone had suggested sending someone over until she arrived: a California

DOJ guy she knew well. I'd said no. *Only her*. And apparently *he* was the "once upon a time" guy she'd brought up before my interview at the fire station.

"We're going to meet up tonight after we get a handle on this," she added.

As exciting as the idea of getting a handle on this was, I was preoccupied by the parallels her situation had with my own. Could. Not. Help it.

"Meet up? You're not leading him on, are you?"

"No. I'm going to get Kevin to understand that long distance never works." She stepped out of the booth and cracked her neck. "And hey, he might be able to help with this case."

Next, Boone took Wolfe into the belltower to check out the contents of the safe. She came back down, eyes alight. She shot me a quick smile and told us the plan.

"I have maybe two evidence bags in my car, about yea big," she made a paperback-sized rectangle with her hands, "and I have to think about security and chain of custody. The evidence is secure and transportable in the safe, so we'll leave it there until it's processed to intake. Let's get it down."

Wolfe set the chain hoist down between us, gestured at Hallenbeck, who was leaning on his cane, and then held out his cuffed hands dramatically.

"Might need these."

"Fine," she said, and shot me a sharp look. "I'm going to supervise and make some calls, but if anything happens, it's on you, Jonesy."

I put on my honor grad smile and gave her a thumbs-up. *On*

me?

Boone uncuffed him and we worked up a sweat getting the safe down to ground level. Unbolting it from the belltower floor, hooking up the chains and hoist, and lowering it by hand onto a furniture dolly. *Crrrrk.* We all winced as the side scraped the corner of the belltower, leaving a swooping mark on the metal. *Thunk.* The weight of the safe pressed the dolly wheels into the damp ground at the base of the belltower. Hallenbeck helped as much as he could, and Boone watched us and made calls. I hoped she knew what she was doing.

"How much does this weigh?" I grunted, pulling the laden dolly out of the muck.

"Two-twenty. I wanted to go heavier but this is what fit under the bell. That's why I bolted it down," Wolfe said, breathing hard.

My phone beeped. We pushed the dolly onto solid ground and I took out the phone. It was an alert for the motion sensor.

"Hey! Motion sensor's triggered," I said. Boone took the phone away from her ear. "Is this you?"

"Not sure. What's the sensor say?"

"Just that something triggered it," I said.

"Could be…an animal…friendlies…or hostiles."

As Boone raised an eyebrow at Hallenbeck, the throb of a car engine filtered through the trees. The eyebrow came down.

"Get inside," she said. "Just in case."

We went. We were on the south, or far side, of the church, and the road and parking lot were on the north side. Boone—and I had to hand it to her—circled around the building instead of going through, making sure she didn't draw attention to the three of us inside. Wolfe and I peered out from the bottom sills of stained-glass windows. Hallenbeck struggled with his cane, which was sticking through a ratty piece of carpet.

A gray sedan with tinted windows came up the road and into the lot. A man and a woman stepped out and waved at Boone.

"Stay there!" Boone shouted. Her right hand went to her side.

They stayed. The man was slender but muscled. He looked in his 30s, but his hair was fully silver. Richard Gere hair. He wore slacks, a polo shirt, and had a gun and badge on his belt. The woman was stocky and masculine, with a buzzcut. Her bottom half was blocked by the hood of the car, but her polo shirt made me think she had a badge and gun too. Richard Gere held up his badge and it glinted in the sun.

That was fast.

"Detective Curione, Mt. Shasta P.D.," he said. "Heard you got a 10-29-F?"

"A 10-16 now," she said as she walked over.

"Agent Boone, right?" Curione smiled and held out his hand.

"In the flesh. Did County call this in?"

She clasped his offered hand. He twisted her wrist, and as she teetered forward he whipped his gun out with his left hand. *Pop-pop.* Boone's head kicked back from the bullets before I realized what I was seeing.

CHAPTER SIXTEEN

The world was vague rainbow light. Was I breathing? Was my heart even beating? My back thumped the panel of a pew. The smells of must and sawdust. My breath caught in my throat. I was here. The world came into focus: beyond the sun-struck stained glass, Boone was a lifeless lump in the church parking lot. The silver-haired shooter—"Detective Curione"—was stalking toward the church with the butch woman, and a third gunman stepped out of the sedan behind them. This was real.

"Get down!" I hissed, yanking Wolfe below the window frame. Hallenbeck was already on the floor, his cane still stuck in rotten flooring.

"Was...it her?" he asked. He hadn't seen it.

I nodded and crawled over, helping him get the cane unstuck.

"Fuck fuck fuck fuck fuck..." Wolfe murmured, wide-eyed

and pale.

"You two go out there." I pointed to a door in the south transept, whispering quickly. "Take the safe, load it up. I'm gonna make some noise in the narthex to draw their attention away."

I peered out a window. Richard Gere—"Curione"—motioned to his counterparts. He moved to circle around the church from one direction, and Butch went toward the opposite corner. She carried an Uzi and had tattoos on her knuckles. The third gunman stayed, keeping the entire north side of the church in view. He looked like a rat, with a long nose, a sloping forehead, and no chin. He had an AR-15.

"Now! Before they get around."

"Stay…low," Hallenbeck hissed as they moved.

I dashed in the narthex, slid next to Wolfe's generator, and pressed the start button. Nothing happened. Was it fueled? Was the battery shot?

I shot a glance down the nave. Hallenbeck was rolling the safe to the designated door, alone, while Wolfe was climbing out the south transept window we'd come through the first night—saving himself. *Bastard.*

I didn't have time to troubleshoot the genny. The table saw was heavy and had some planks on it. I threw it over.

It crashed on the floor, the planks thunking loudly. I didn't have any real weapons. The rifle, my tricks n' treats, and *everything else* was in the motorhome. We'd stowed it all away to avoid issues with Boone. I grabbed a two-by-four and hid by the entrance. Just in time.

Butch burst into the narthex, eyes blazing, and I broke the

two-by-four on her face. She *whuffed* and fell on her ass, blood gushing from her nose. Grabbing another plank, I closed the narthex-to-nave doors behind me, barred them to shut her in, and ran back down the nave to Hallenbeck. I saw Wolfe through the windows: he ran into the motorhome. *Fucking bastard.*

Pop-pop. Tink. Pop-pop-pop. Bullets snapped past me, smashing through glass, embedding in wood, spanging off brick—Ratface shooting from outside. I met Hallenbeck's gaze and bulled the safe out the transept door, pulling him with me. The dolly listed, but we righted it onto the pathway and rolled it into a windowless corner. For a matter of seconds, we were protected from Ratface by the bricks.

Angry shouts and a cry of pain sounded from the motorhome. Wolfe and Curione.

Hallenbeck smiled grimly and held up a jangling keychain. "Wolfe's."

"Nice." I snatched them. Hustling, we rolled the safe to his truck. *Be tough to fit the safe through the motorhome door anyway*, I thought.

A wet smack from the motorhome.

"Thank you, sir, may I have another?" Wolfe cackled.

"You know who sent us. You know what will happen if you don't cooperate." Another wet smack. The motorhome windows, which we'd left open, now gave us a very clear sound picture of Curione interrogating Wolfe with his fists. "Where's your 'insurance policy'?" Curione's voice was calm and cold. He had Wolfe, but *we* had his insurance policy.

"One…two…three," I grunted, and Hallenbeck and I lifted

the safe into the truck bed and carefully closed the tailgate.

"Where's Jones?" Curione asked.

They knew about me…they had known about Boone too…

Wolfe didn't answer. The thump of a hit and a grunt. Then another cackle.

"Do you fucking *like* it?" Curione asked.

Hallenbeck was red-faced and tottering, even with his cane. I helped him into the passenger seat and got behind the wheel.

"You okay?"

He waved stiffly.

"Fucking…go."

I turned the key and the engine rumbled to life. Wolfe wouldn't last long. He always caved. And once he caved, Curione would kill him. We had the safe with Wolfe's evidence. I could hit the gas and leave this shitshow behind. Find a haven, turn the evidence over to the authorities. We didn't need Wolfe.

In the rearview, Butch came around the corner of the church to the north side. I shifted into reverse. The direction where the killers were.

Mason, are you really gonna risk the safe, risk your life, *for this asshole?*

Yes, Mason, apparently I am.

"Duck and hold on," I said, and stomped the gas.

"The…fuck…"

The truck barreled backward, I turned the wheel a *mite*, and the back bumper glanced off the back corner of the motorhome. The truck rocked—but so did the motorhome. I socked it into park and jumped out, bounding into the motorhome as Butch sprayed the Uzi.

Tik tik tik! The bullets plunked into the fiberglass shell of the Starcraft.

Curione disentangled himself from a bloody-faced Wolfe, both of them on the floor because of the impact. Curione's eyes darted from me to the tinking shell.

"Friendly fire! Friendly fire!" he shouted.

The bullets stopped. But not before I'd taken his gun from the kitchen table and leveled it at his head.

"Out."

He grimaced.

"Get the fuck out."

He clambered out, hands up. I looked past him through the doorway. Butch stood at a safe distance, Uzi low but ready. Next to the truck, Ratface had Hallenbeck in the mud at gunpoint. The bottom dropped out of my stomach.

"Let him go." I pointed my weapon at Curione. "Exchange."

Butch slowly raised the Uzi.

"Keep that fucking muzzle down," I shouted. "It moves another inch and I blow his head off."

Butch grimaced and let it drop. Ratface looked at Curione. Curione, eyes narrowed, shook his head minutely.

I fired two shots in front of his feet.

"Now. Him for him." We weren't getting out of here with the safe. We'd be lucky to get out of here with our lives.

Curione spat, then nodded at Ratface.

Ratface pushed Hallenbeck away and I kept my sights trained on Curione until Hallenbeck was at the door. He staggered onto the step extension and struggled up the deep door well. "Help him!" I hissed at Wolfe. Wolfe pulled him inside. "Get the rifle." Hallenbeck took up his rifle, sat on the floor, and pointed it out the door. I handed the pistol to Wolfe and ran to the driver's seat—the keys were in the ignition. Wolfey had gotten real close.

"Keep it…outboard—point…pointed at them," Hallenbeck told Wolfe, and they pointed their weapons out as I turned the ignition and spurred the motorhome down the hill. It jostled over the lumpy, sloped terrain.

"Weapons free!" Curione roared. *Tunk-tunk-tunk-tunk!* Bullets peppered the Starcraft with abandon. Fiberglass was supposed to stand up well to bullets, wasn't it? *Crack! Pop!* Hallenbeck and Wolfe returned fire. The bouncing of the vehicle probably fucked their shots, but it just might fuck the enemies' too.

Scraping the front undercarriage, the motorhome came to level ground at the bottom and I pulled a wicked turn, almost tipping us over.

"Their…vehicle!" Hallenbeck shouted, and the pair laid fire down in a new direction.

In one sideview mirror, the gray sedan sank onto two flat tires, its windshield splintered.

In the other sideview mirror, Wolfe's safe-laden truck disappeared behind a knoll.

"Fuck," I growled, trying to and failing to spit out the brassy, acrid taste of gunfire.

Tunk-tunk! We made it to the opposite side of the church and the shooters lost line of sight. I felt the asphalt of the parking lot grip the tires and I blasted down the road.

"How we doing back there?" I asked, panting and jittery.

I glanced back. A double spiderweb of cracks glowed in the back window. Hallenbeck and Wolfe sat around the kitchen table. Hallenbeck rattled pills out of a canister into his mouth. Wolfe was ashen, and the hand he held to his ribs was covered in blood.

He'd caught a bullet.

My first thought, fucked up as it may have been, was, *We should've left with the safe when we had the chance.*

Wolfe slumped over in the seat.

CHAPTER SEVENTEEN

I pushed the pedal to the floor, urging the behemoth south toward the nearest hospital. Hallenbeck had his first aid kit out and was pressing gauze on Wolfe's chest.

"What's your EMT level?" I asked.

"Does...does it matter?" He held up a stiff hand. No fine motor control.

I grimaced and he went back to putting pressure on the wound.

"Is that all you can do?"

"Yep," he replied.

Sweat salting my eyes, I saw a truck stop just in time and burned rubber taking the exit. I slammed into park behind a container truck—it would keep us from view of the highway—and slid out of my seat.

Wolfe's black shirt would have made it difficult to see how

much he was bleeding, except the gauze was soaked and the kitchen table was splattered crimson. I peeled Wolfe from the fiberglass seat. The entry wound was in his back, a dribbling perforation. In front, the exit wound was gushing carnage. His pulse was low and spotty. His breathing was shallow and he was unconscious.

This was way beyond EMT-Basic.

Breathe. Think.

I taped a homeostatic dressing over the entry wound on his back. One down. Hallenbeck had been using regular gauze on Wolfe's chest instead of the blood-clotting homeostatics. I hoped it was because of an inability to open the packets, and not because he'd chosen less effective aid.

"Help me get him supine," I said, and Hallenbeck helped me lower him to the floor, face-up. To make room, I swept aside the mess of shredded greens, shattered terra cotta, and loose soil that used to be my potted herbs. Layering homeostatics over the soaked pieces, I took over the attempt to stop Wolfe's bleeding. The blood was bright red, with bubbles fizzing out. Warm and sticky on my hands, sweet and metallic to my nose.

How'd they find us? Was it me? Jasmine? Hallenbeck? I motioned Hallenbeck at my tricks n' treats.

"There's aluminum foil in there. Get it out."

He got out two thick aluminum foil pockets. A poor man's Faraday sleeves.

"For our phones." I had no idea how that man, "Curione," had found us, so we had to take every precaution. I handed Hallenbeck my cell phone. I didn't know if his phone had a physical SIM or eSIM, and this was the fastest way to make them both disappear from the grid. Plus, we might need them later.

Hallenbeck put our phones in the pockets and folded the aluminum over.

I kept one hand on Wolfe's chest and used the other to take Burner #1 from the bag.

"We need help."

"Ortiz?" he asked.

I shook my head. "The police."

Hallenbeck smacked the new phone out of my hand.

"Ow!"

"Not yet. Not…safe."

I glared at him, my hand stinging. The man had some strength when he needed to, that was for sure. I forced myself to breathe in and out. He was right. The last cop I called was dead. It wasn't safe for us *or* the cops.

"Fine. Help me with him. Guide me."

Hallenbeck picked up the burner instead. It had locked. He glanced at the still-unconscious Wolfe, but he was preoccupied with the view of the shipping container outside the window.

"The code?" He tapped the blood-smeared lock screen.

"What are you doing?"

"The track…tracker."

The GPS tracker inside the rear bumper of Wolfe's truck. The truck that now had the safe in its bed. Hallenbeck and Wolfe had given the Curione crew's sedan two flat tires and a windshield splintered by bullet holes. Even if they fixed the tires, that windshield would attract attention. They couldn't risk being pulled over by CHP. Chances are, they'd use the truck to take the safe for themselves. It was conveniently loaded up. And every burner in my tricks n' treats bag had the tracker app installed.

We were only a few miles from McGreary and the church. From where they'd be.

"We can...go after them," Hallenbeck said, voicing my thoughts.

The evidence in that safe was damning and Curione's crew didn't know about the tracker. If we could catch *them* by surprise, we could take the safe back and get it to the authorities.

Wolfe's pale skin took on a blueish tint. *Cyanoxis,* or something like that. I didn't remember exactly what it was called, but it meant he wasn't getting enough oxygen. His breaths were faster and shallower, with a wheeze in them.

"We can go after them," Hallenbeck repeated.

"One thing at a time," I said.

"How long...'til they ditch the truck?" Hallenbeck asked.

If it were up to me, I'd move the safe to a fresh vehicle and ditch the original as soon as I could. But I didn't tell him that.

"We have a short...window," Hallenbeck said, answering his own question.

"What about *his* window?"

Blue and catatonic, Wolfe was oblivious to the debate.

Hallenbeck shrugged.

"Help me stabilize him and I'll tell you the code," I said.

Hallenbeck frowned and knelt down. He lifted my hand off the wound and used the homeostatic stack to wipe a gummy clot of blood. A rush of air tickled my fingers, and with my hands away, I could hear a sucking sound as Wolfe breathed.

"Need…needed a burp," he said. "Tape some plastic…over it."

I readied bandage tape and the plastic wrap the dressings came in. It was all we had.

"On the…exhale," Hallenbeck directed.

I placed the dressing over the wound as Wolfe exhaled.

His breathing remained shallow, but it steadied. His skin seemed to turn less blue.

"He needs a hos…hospital," he said.

"You think?" I massaged my scalp, waxing my hair with blood. "If he's admitted, they might find him and finish the job."

Hallenbeck shrugged. It was halting and slow, but it was a shrug.

"You did your best. It's more…than he deserves." He gestured to the truck stop outside. "We…leave him here, a trucker will call an ambulance. Keeps…us out of it."

And we'd have a chance to catch up to Curione and take back the safe. Boone's death wouldn't be for nothing, and it would prove that my life was worth a damn. Take the time to get Wolfe to a hospital and we could lose that chance. My hands trembled from crashing adrenaline. I massaged the back of my neck, torn.

I was no doctor, but I'd heard the first part of the Hippocratic Oath. First, do no harm. I was pretty sure abandoning a man at a truck stop with a sucking chest wound was doing harm.

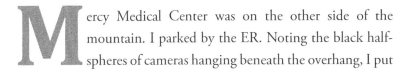

ercy Medical Center was on the other side of the mountain. I parked by the ER. Noting the black half-spheres of cameras hanging beneath the overhang, I put on a medical mask to hide my face. They were a common sight in waiting rooms these days, so nothing suspicious there. The gunshot victim though…

A bolt of pain lanced up my back as I lifted Wolfe off the floor of the motorhome. Hallenbeck held the door against me, Burner #1 in his hand. *Asshole.*

"Code," he said.

"6-8-8-5-9," I told him.

He struggled to tap the numbers in, his fine motor control deficit hampering his efforts. I almost snatched it and did it myself, but then he got it. The phone unlocked and he got out of the way.

I plodded through the automatic doors with my back screaming. Wolfe's eyes snapped open beneath the bright fluorescence.

"My penance…" he wheezed, then passed out again.

In the waiting room sat a teenager with road-rashed forearms, an old couple, and a woman with a coughing baby. They all stared at us.

"Sir…" the nurse behind the glass began.

"Gunshot victim," I said.

A Filipino nurse behind her moved quickly. Seconds later, she was pushing a wheeled gurney out of swinging double doors over to us. I placed Wolfe on it as gently as I could. He didn't move and made no sound other than his wheezing breaths.

The Filipino nurse—no, her ID badge said M.D. on it—took a clipboard off the gurney.

"Two thoracic gunshot wounds," I told her, and the doctor started writing. "Entry is in the back, exit in the front. Lung is probably perforated, wound was sucking and he had trouble breathing."

"Patient history?" the doctor asked, looking up from the form.

I should've been ready for that question, but I wasn't. I took a second to think but remained at a loss.

"Unknown."

"Patient name?"

"Please do what you can for him," I said, ignoring the question I *had* been ready for. I took one last look at Wolfe's bloody supine form and marched out before she could call anybody.

Hallenbeck was in the driver seat, the phone glowing in a dash holder. He shouldn't have been in the driver's seat—but we needed to get the fuck out of here. The intake nurse was probably on the phone with the cops already.

I climbed into the passenger seat and he hit the gas. The map on the phone showed a blinking dot moving south down the 5.

"How far away are they?" I asked.

"Eighty miles," he muttered.

There was the possibility that Curione and his crew would get right down to it, tearing open the safe and destroying the evidence. But it's not what I'd do. If *I* thought the safe contained evidence against me, I'd want to find out for myself what it was, and the only person I'd trust with it was Ortiz. I doubted Marshall had an Ortiz. He had hired guns.

"Does Marshall trust his hired guns to open the safe and examine the evidence themselves?" I wondered aloud.

"Don't…think so," Hallenbeck said, following my train of thought.

Meaning we needed to catch them and get the safe before

they delivered it to Marshall, and we were 80 miles behind in a lumbering motorhome.

"Lost our…best shot."

He wasn't wrong. Stabilizing Wolfe and taking him to the hospital had cost us. Wolfe wasn't even a good man—that's why he'd been sweating away in that church covered in scars.

Not worth missing our shot at Marshall for. But…*before* he panicked and tried to abandon us, he had been trying to do the right thing, handing over the safe and himself to Boone…

How do you know what the right thing is?

It was a question I would've asked the old Hallenbeck. But I knew I wouldn't like the answer of this new one, whose disgusted face shone like a shattered moon in the blue light of the phone.

CHAPTER EIGHTEEN

FROM: ASAC, FBI FIELD OFFICE LOS ANGELES
TO: ADIC, FBI FIELD OFFICE SACRAMENTRO
SUBJECT: MCGREARY/DEL RIO INCIDENTS

Special Agent Tina Prescott of the California DOJ's Bureau of Investigation was dismayed to find that fellow agent Kevin Luo had gotten to Mercy Medical before her. She thought it was for the best that she didn't have a partner, but someone needed to reign *Kevin* in. He was a man on a mission, and if he accomplished it, everything would be royally ducked. Yes, ducked. Prescott thought vulgarity was as hateful as it was commonplace.

She'd failed to nip this rash situation in the bud at the broken-down church. She had found him in the confessional, hugging his knees. The booth was startingly intact compared to the rest of it. Prescott had felt the smoothness of the wood, noted the sawdust in the nave. Not intact. Recently rebuilt.

Kevin's face had been puffy, his eyes red. Through a broken stained-glass window, the coroner loaded Jasmine Boone's body into his van. Prescott edged around to block the view from Luo's line of sight.

"Is she the one you told me about?" Prescott asked. She meant, "the one who got away," but figured saying that would just make it worse.

Luo nodded.

That complicated things. His feelings for the parole agent had bordered on—and maybe crossed the line into—obsession.

"We had plans to meet up tonight."

"I'm sorry," she said. She was.

"Let's get you back to the office. I'll keep tabs on this and keep you posted—you need some distance."

Luo laughed grimly. "Yeah. Sure."

She helped him up and they marched to their cars.

"Are you okay to drive?" she asked.

He answered by flipping up the screen of his dash computer.

"Who did they say they like for this?"

"Kevin," she warned.

"Who?"

She considered not telling him. But he'd find out anyway, and then he wouldn't trust her. She couldn't risk being out of the loop.

"Mason Jones. He has a record."

Luo had nodded. "I'll catch up with you later," he'd said, and drove off.

Now, Prescott had caught up with *him*—at Mercy Medical,

Mt. Shasta. Luo was accosting a thickset man in scrubs outside the John Doe's room. Prescott flicked her eyes over the man, noting his ID tag and stance. He was a nurse named Dean, and Dean wasn't going to take crap from anyone. He blocked Luo from the room.

"I want to talk to your supervisor. You're interfering with an investigation."

"My supervisor is on a break, and you haven't shown me even a scrap of paper that says you can see this patient. He isn't even conscious."

"We can fix that."

Goodness, Kevin, Prescott thought.

The nurse picked up a clipboard.

"The hell are you doing?"

"Documenting this conversation, sir."

Prescott beelined in and grabbed Luo's arm.

"Situational awareness, Agent Luo," she hissed. He allowed her to pull him away and she led him outside.

She stood across from him in the red and white glare of the ER sign and studied his face. He was *gone*.

"Snap out of it."

"Are you here to nag me or watch my back?" he asked.

"I'm here to keep you from getting yourself into trouble."

"He murdered Jasmine."

"He's a person of interest," she said. "We don't have all the facts. That's why you ask questions." He was acting like a two-bit Brady-list bonehead, not a special agent of the California Department of Justice.

"He doesn't talk to cops."

"How do you know that?"

"Talked to an investigator from LAC, an Agent Brown. They found Jones covered in buckets of his own brother's blood and he wouldn't even finger the guy who did it. That tells me everything I need to know about him."

This was getting out of control. What else didn't she know?

"What about his cooperation with LASD? The Marshall case?"

Luo was surprised. "The *what* case? Where'd you hear about that?"

Prescott waved dismissively. She was always prepared, like a Girl Scout was supposed to be. *People never remember that 'Be Prepared' was also the Girl Scouts' motto*, she grumbled internally.

"The man who killed Jasmine does not go back to prison with a TV in his cell and three squares a day. No way. Let's save the taxpayers some money on this one." He chuckled bitterly.

At least he trusted her enough to tell her he planned to kill Jones.

She could manage Kevin. She had to.

"I have your back, okay?"

He nodded.

"Let's roll. I have an idea," she said.

Doctor Anna Del Rosario heard the exchange. If she had been smoking, they would've known she was there, but for two months now, every time she got the urge she slapped a patch on her shoulder, sat in the shadow of the ER sign, and texted her husband Jeff until it passed.

Anna tried to quiet her breathing as the pair walked away. She wiped her palms on her scrubs—they hadn't been this sweaty since her first week of residency.

Her first thought was: *None of my business.*

Her second was: *Do no harm.*

Those agents were going to kill that man.

She had seen Jones bring in the John Doe. He had bandaged his wounds and stayed to describe his condition. Very responsible for a murderer. His bandages had occluded the lung perforation and probably saved the Doe's life. Of course, it was possible that the Doe was an accomplice to the murder the agents had mentioned… or maybe Jones wasn't a murderer.

Anna wiped her hands—again—and marched inside. She decided against texting Jeff. He'd probably try to talk her out of this. First, she got their names from Dean. Agent Luo and Agent Prescott. She filed that away in her mind. Next, she gently tapped the John Doe awake. *You unprofessional bitch*, she scolded herself.

He blinked groggily at her, his mouth and nose covered by the ventilator mask.

"How are you feeling?"

He wiggled his hand. The man was struggling to stay cognizant.

She handed her patient a pen and a clipboard with his intake form on it. The height, weight, and other biometrics had been filled in, but there was no name. Dean had used a whole separate page to detail his identifying marks—all those self-injuries.

"What's your name?"

He shook his head.

Given the brands, scars, and his gunshot wound, Anna wasn't surprised that he didn't want to give it.

"Do you remember what happened?" she asked.

He nodded.

It was clear from the ritual scarification that this patient was a troubled soul. Could she even trust him?

"The man who brought you in," the patient nodded in understanding, "do you know him?"

A rattle from the man. A laugh? He winced, then nodded again.

He was in pain. She should stop. But she'd already gone this far…

"Did he do this to you?"

He shook his head. Then scribbled on the chart.

HIS FAULT THO.

"Did he kill that woman?"

He shook his head.

NOT A KILLER. The mask fogged up and he grimaced in pain. He shrugged sadly, underlined *HIS FAULT*, and added, *ASSHOLE.* He put down the pen and closed his eyes. Whether it was from emotion or pain, Anna wasn't sure.

This was some complicated shit.

Another rattle from his throat, but this time it sounded like a sigh. Doe opened his eyes and picked the pen back up.

SAVED MY LIFE, he wrote.

Muscles Anna hadn't even realized were clenched went loose. She breathed deep to stay on her feet. And then her hands went clammy again.

"There are two California DOJ agents gunning for him," she said. "And not to arrest him."

Doe's eyes widened. He was struggling to stay conscious. He made a shaky circle on the form.

"I don't understand."

He tapped the circle. It was—loosely—around the word PHONE.

Doctor Del Rosario brought out her phone. Before handing it to him, she crossed herself. The patient's eyes crinkled in pleasure at that.

Please God, let me be doing the right thing, she prayed.

CHAPTER NINETEEN

I woke with a start to see farmland unfurling from both sides of the 5. We were out of the mountains again. The motorhome smelled sickly sweet and earthy. Slapping the back of my head and stretching, I tried to shake off the drained, adrenaline crash feeling. I'd fallen asleep and left a man with a brain injury at the wheel—and he was probably exhausted too. A 5 o'clock shadow pebbled his face, his clothes were brown with Wolfe's blood, but he didn't show any signs of exhaustion. His eyes were intent even as he grimaced and fought his spasticity to pass a slow-moving van. The sight brought a fullness to my chest that surprised me.

Chronic pain was a bitch. Every day I gritted through twangs and throbs from my hand, and here was Hallenbeck, moving through it all while every movement brought pain. Physically, he was playing the hand he'd been dealt damn well. And he had a good head on his shoulders. I trusted that head. I didn't trust his heart. It was stupid, me wanting him to be who he used to be. Childish.

"I should take over," I told him.

"Piss...and hydrate first," he said.

That sounded a lot more like the old Hallenbeck, the man who looked out for his troops. I guess he was still in there.

I *did* have to piss, and I shuffled to the bathroom, the floor vibrating under my feet. I brought back two waters and eyed the tracking app.

The screen glow highlighted a dried blood smear, but beneath it, the dot blinked. Still heading south. Curione's crew didn't know we were tracking them and could afford to continue using Wolfe's truck for a while. We didn't have the same luxury.

"We need a new car."

Hallenbeck grunted but didn't argue. He knew I was right.

Curione and his crew would get even farther ahead, but they'd see us coming in *this* rig. That, and it was connected to the drop-off of a gunshot victim.

"Don't think we should rent one," I said. The more we stayed off the grid, the better.

"Me neither."

"Well, shit."

"Shit," he agreed.

"About me being a crook..." I began. I was *supposed* to be done with all that.

"You...want to steal one?"

I didn't hear any disapproval in his voice and winced internally. That was more in line with the new and improved Hallenbeck.

I looked at the navigation app. We weren't far from Redding. Because *of course* we weren't.

"Not exactly," I told him.

She was never around when she was tweaking. She came home for the comedown. She'd say she was under the weather, but just because I was 13 didn't mean I was stupid. That week, *I* was the one who was under the weather—with the goddamn flu, no less. Caleb was at football camp even though we'd never been able to afford that kind of thing. Years later, he told me he paid for it by selling a catalytic converter he'd stolen.

Shivering under two blankets and the blast of a space heater, I heaved up the raw ramen I'd eaten a few minutes ago into a Tupperware. It was almost full. The cooking pot would hold more, but it was crusted with mac n cheese and made me want to hurl more than I already had. I lumbered to the bathroom and flushed the vomit, holding onto the toilet for minutes or an hour until the dizziness passed. Sweat pouring off my scalp, I was roasting now. Spinning and roasting. I was a goddamn rotisserie chicken.

Freezing cold then burning hot? Did that mean I had a fever? I palmed my forehead. Hot. Maybe. It was hard to tell. I tried to push myself up, but my hands slipped on the toilet bowl. I hoped because of sweat.

I had never been this sick. I needed medicine or a doctor. I went on all fours and got to my feet somewhere in the living room, like an Animorph returning to human form. WWJBD. What Would Jake Berenson Do? He wouldn't just lie there and stare at the ceiling, that's for sure. When had I laid down again?

The crack in the ceiling was a spider that skittered down the walls and burrowed into my stomach. I clawed at my belly, drawing blood from the lip of my belly button. There was no spider.

Am I dying? I wondered.

Body aching, head pounding, I staggered the length of our single-wide to the master bedroom. The air was like ice. I'd always hated how small this trailer was, now I hated how large.

She was in bed with her eyes closed. She tugged the covers over her head and turned away. Not asleep. She did this a lot: lying there but not sleeping. *If you can't sleep, why not take care of your son?*

"I don't feel good, Mom."

"Not now, Macie," she murmured. I was too out of it to register irritation at the nickname. "It's your useless teachers. They never make your classmates cover their mouths, and they're coughing and sneezing all over the place. I've seen it," she said. "Drink water and eat some crackers, it'll pass."

"I keep throwing up."

"We probably got the same bug. It'll pass for both of us."

"Mom."

I pulled the covers down from her face and put her hand on my forehead. That was something moms were supposed to do.

"I think I'm really sick."

"I'm sorry, bud. There's some Nyquil in the cupboard with Caleb's protein stuff."

Maybe I'd missed it. I trudged there, and now I was on fire again. Emptied the cupboard. No Nyquil. No medicine. Just protein powders and glowing ooze, the kind that turns turtles into walking-talking ninjas. Swaying, I blinked at the ooze. Turns out it was just pre-workout boosters.

I'm going to die, I thought. Then... *No.*

I had $25 cash hidden in the *Crash Bandicoot* disc container. I'd had to change the hiding spot after Mom raided my underwear drawer. I was saving for the new *Final Fantasy* game, but hey, I was dying.

The world outside was spotty. I wasn't sure if it was day or night. Cars and traffic lights moved fuzzily and time was out of sync. I almost got hit by a car.

Somehow, I made it to the 7-11. Guzzled sports drinks right out of the window fridge, grabbed cartons and bottles labeled *SEVERE COLD/FLU* and took them to the counter. The man at the register said I wasn't old enough. He was nice about it, even though his beard was made of snakes. I threw up on the floor and the snakes cried out in irritation. You'd think they'd hiss.

I don't remember how I got home, but I had flu meds and Gatorade. I washed down a pill and threw it all back up. *How do I make it stop? How can I ever get better?*

My eyelids became lead. Even sitting up in bed was exhausting. *Sleep.*

Goosebumps that had nothing to do with flu chills prickled across my arms. My chest tightened and it wasn't because I had to hurl.

What if I fell asleep and never woke up?

I needed help, and Mom couldn't. Wouldn't.

I had the cordless in my lap. I blinked rapidly to get the rubber buttons in focus, then pressed down.

9.

1.

I stopped.

Who would take care of Caleb if they took Mom away? I wondered.

I put the phone down and slipped into black and red fever dreams.

B ehind the wheel again, I braked the motorhome in front of a storefront: JONESY FURNITURE RESTORATION & CUSTOMIZATION. Proprietor: Kathleen "Kit" Jones. Kit had mentioned her new digs in a voicemail she left Caleb four or so years ago.

Jonesy. Boone would've loved that. *"My favorite absconsion risk."* My insides twisted as she crumpled from the gunshots in my mind's eye. She'd frustrated the hell out of me, but she'd been *good*. She'd tried to *help*.

It damn sure wouldn't be for nothing.

"She lives in the apartment over it. The car's gotta be around here somewhere," I said.

"You think…it's not stealing if it's…if it's from family?"

"Basically." *Especially in this case,* I thought, *because this bitch stole money I earned mowing lawns to score crank.* "Let's just say that letting us take the car is the least she can do."

CHAPTER TWENTY

I parked the motorhome down the street and we made our way quietly back to the shop, me with my tricks n' treats on my back, the late afternoon sun giving us slinking Slender Man shadows. There wasn't a garage in front or on the side, and nothing was parked on the street in front of it. We circled around to the back alley. Bingo. A gated carport held an oldish Toyota pickup truck. She'd always liked Toyotas.

"How are your hips and shoulders doing?"

"They…hurt. Thanks…for reminding me."

"What I'm here for." I moved to the back door, cinching the pack straps until they dug into my clavicles, loosening them, then tightening them again. I told myself that this was what we had to do.

Hallenbeck limped after. We'd be in bad shape if we had to

make a run for it.

"You're not going to lock…smith the gate and hotwire it?"

"It's old, but not that old." I raked my eyes over the truck. "Anything past the mid '90s has locking mechanisms and all kinds of shit you have to know for that model and year. We're breaking in and taking the keys."

Hallenbeck eyed the truck.

"While she's…home."

"Yeah."

I handed him a tub of multi-purpose grease from the duffel and pointed at the wheels for the gate tracks.

"Get to work on those. We don't want it squeaking."

I thought he'd complain but he just nodded and got to work.

Shoulders tight, scalp itchy with tension, I locksmithed the back door as quietly as I could. The bottom step creaked. I thought feathery thoughts and glided up the rest without a sound. Peering over the threshold, the stairs opened up to a hallway with a bedroom straight ahead, a kitchen to the side, and behind, a living room, where she was.

I wasn't ready for how small and old she looked. Kit sat on couch with a mousy white girl about my age, reading passages aloud from a teal book. I recognized it as something NA. At La Cuenca Conservation Camp, I'd lied about being an addict to cover up a *different* lie. The girl was probably her sponsee. Kit had muffins and ice waters on the coffee table.

A sliver of the kitchen was visible from my vantage point. An edge of a countertop with a black lump that might be a purse. If it was, that's where the keys would be. But I couldn't cross the hallway to the kitchen without them seeing me. Maybe if I crawled? I turned to look at them again.

Kit smiled at something Mousy said. And then *clapped* at something else.

The banister creaked in my hands—I forced myself to relax a white-knuckle grip. I should be getting the keys, but my blood was burning and all I could see was Kit fawning over this girl.

She touched the girl's water glass, noting it was room temp. I ducked as she bustled by, getting ice and fresh water from the fridge. *How sweet.* I clung to the steps as she brought the drink back to the girl.

The girl thanked her and apologized about something, and Kit pish-poshed it. I peered up at them again, angling myself behind a sofa.

"…but it was three in the morning," Mousy said.

"Doesn't matter. Call or text anytime, I'm here for you."

I'm here for you, little mouse. Fuck me and Caleb, her actual children. Couldn't have her shit together for us. A bolt of pain flared in my jaw—I was grinding my teeth.

Now she was capable of being a mother.

The bottom step creaked—ripping my eyes away to Hallenbeck at the bottom. He made a *Well?* gesture and tapped his watch. How long had I been watching them? Standing there like a childish idiot instead of doing what I came to do?

Snapping out of it, I considered the task at hand. The living room had a window to the street.

"Firework poppers. In the bag," I whispered down to him. "Across the street. Distraction."

Hallenbeck nodded and made a point of stepping over the creaky bottom step on his way out. You had to respect him. Despite everything, he was clutch.

I stayed below the stairway threshold while I waited. I didn't need to watch any more of that. It was only a few minutes, but it seemed longer.

Snap! Snap! The fireworks went off in the street, and I prairie-dogged up to watch Kit and Mousy go to the window. I treaded lightly and quickly into the kitchen, which would keep me out of their sight unless they came down the hallway. The black lump *was* a purse, and I plunged my hand into it, rummaging. Keys! The keychain had a Toyota key and five others on the ring—one had to be for the carport gate.

Snap! Snap!

Clutch. He knew to keep it going without me having told him. I poked my head into the hallway, but they were sitting back down.

"Teenagers," Kit said.

I crawled on the hallway floor, hoping the sofa across from them would give me some cover. Not daring to look up, I glided down the stairs.

Clunk. The carport gate unlocked with the fourth key.

"We'll transfer what we need from the motorhome and dump it somewhere that doesn't give a clue where we're going," I said, thinking aloud.

"I…have some ideas," Hallenbeck said.

Skrrt. The carport gate squealed once as we pulled it, then rolled quietly the rest of the way along the track.

Brrrm. The six cylinders came to life with a twist of the rubber-gripped key. A diffuser choked the cabin with an eye-watering lavender scent. Hallenbeck lurched into the passenger seat with a grunt and a wince. I put it in *Drive.*

Crack! Kit stood in front of the truck with a shotgun she'd just fired into the air. Hallenbeck ducked and I stomped on the brake pedal even though we hadn't moved.

She pointed the shotgun at us. "Don't move!"

Her grip slipped.

"Mason?"

"Hey." I waved awkwardly.

Kit let the shotgun muzzle drop to point at the ground.

"What the hell are you doing?"

"We're taking the truck."

"Is everything okay?" The Mousy girl asked from the stairway, eyes so wide she looked even mousier.

"It's fine, sweetie," Kit said. "We'll have to put a pin in this."

"No need, we're leaving," I said.

"Not just yet you're not." Kit squared her stance in front of the truck, daring us to mow down her tiny body. I was already in *Drive.* All I'd have to do was smash the gas…

Face burning, I sighed and put it in *Park.* I used to steal cars for a living and got caught trying to take one by my *mom.*

"Frankie, this is my son, Mason."

Somehow, the girl's eyes got even wider. I wondered what Kit had said about me in meetings. Kit edged to a headlight—barely blocking the truck now, but I'd smack her hip if I gunned it—and motioned Frankie over for a warm hug.

"I'll be fine," Kit told her. "Please call if you need anything."

The girl left.

An awkward silence followed.

"Look…" I began.

The burner phone buzzed from an incoming call. Only one person had the number to the burners. I answered it.

"Hey, man, crazy night. Kind of busy," I said.

"Yo, good you're not using your personal phone," Ortiz said. "Smart. I had to try and get you."

I knew it was smart, but why did he? I glanced at Hallenbeck.

"Really, Mason? We're in the middle of something here!" Kit said.

I ignored her.

"Are you near a TV?" Ortiz asked.

My chest tightened. I told him yes.

"Turn it to Channel 7."

In a trance, I found myself drifting back up the stairs. Kit and Hallenbeck followed me inside. I turned the TV on and went to Channel 7.

Big block letters said *MANHUNT* and a male reporter spoke next to my mugshot, "…in Northern California for a suspect who police believe shot and killed a parole officer. This man, Mason Jones, is considered armed and dangerous."

Beneath my mugshot was more text: Reportedly involved in officer shooting. Wanted for homicide, prohibited use of a weapon, fleeing the scene of a crime.

My heart thudded heavy and slow. My legs turned to rubber—I forced myself to move to keep from collapsing. *Wanted for homicide.*

"According to authorities, Jones, a former convict, may have tricked his former parole agent into meeting him in McGreary, where the shooting took place. Jones was last seen at Mercy Medical Center, Mt. Shasta, in Siskiyou County."

Yeah, because I took a man to the ER *to try to save his life*. Fucking fucking *fuck*. I paced the living room, eyes glued to the screen. Hallenbeck white-knuckled his cane, grimly focused on the TV. Kit looked back and forth between me and the news, twisting a necklace in her fingers.

"They say he also has ties to Los Angeles, where he lives," the reporter continued. "If you have any information on his location, call the number on the screen."

Wanted for homicide. My muscles felt like they'd jump right off my body if I didn't clench every single one of them. *The police are after me and they think I killed Boone.*

CHAPTER TWENTY-ONE

You still there?" Ortiz's voice came tinny from the phone, which I'd forgot I was holding.

"I'm here," I said. In the physical sense, that was true enough. But I was dizzy and outside myself, somehow, at the same time. The reporter had turned it over to the weather lady and I turned it off.

"Think it's time to get out your go bag. I don't know if you're safe," I told him. A shiver of concern broke through the dreamlike state.

"From the police?"

"Marshall's people. They found us and I don't know how. They're the ones that killed Boone."

"Fuck." A clopping sound came over the speaker.

"Stop chewing your nails," I said.

He blew a stormy breath and grunted acknowledgment.

"I gotta go," he said.

"You do. Be safe. And…thanks, brother."

"Always," Ortiz said, and the line went dead.

I took a deep breath, trying to get a hold of myself. Then I screamed.

"Fuck!"

Hallenbeck sank into the couch, sighing.

Kit stared at me with wide eyes.

"What is going on, Mason?"

"Well, I didn't kill anyone," I said. I wasn't even *capable* of killing.

Ding ding! Hallenbeck pulled out a phone, which was receiving multiple texts. It was his *personal* phone.

"Why isn't your phone turned off and wrapped in foil?" I asked. I marched over, face heating. It was all I could do not to smack it out of his hand, just like the bastard had done to me.

"I had to…call my wife earlier… I forgot."

"Well, turn it off."

"Hold your…horses." He handed me the phone. It had a block of texts from an UNKNOWN CALLER, and in the text thread was a video clip of a man in a hospital bed hooked up to a ventilator.

Wolfe.

"He pulled through."

"What now? Someone better tell me what's going on!" Kit shouted.

"Play it," Hallenbeck said.

I slumped down next to him and tapped the video clip. Kit

sidled up behind the couch and watched over our shoulders.

Wolfe waved weakly at the camera and nodded at the person holding it. The camera flipped to the doctor I'd left him with.

"I'm Doctor— I'm a doctor at Mercy Medical and I believe you're in danger."

An icy chill spread over me as she continued, telling me about Special Agents Luo and Prescott from the California DOJ. They were after me, and not to put me in bracelets. They were out for blood, because they believed I was "the man who killed Jasmine." Like the rest of the world now. Had they known her? The doctor made it sound like it was personal.

"I— The patient you brought in wanted you to know. Please… don't make me regret this," the doctor finished. The clip ended.

"What exactly are you involved in?" Kit asked.

I marched down the stairs and into the carport, slamming the back door behind me and sinking to the floor. It was a good question.

Kit opened the door without bothering to knock and knelt beside me. I didn't acknowledge her. *Not now, Macie.* How many times had I heard that?

"What can I do to help?" she asked.

"What?" I granted her a glance. Her hair had almost as much gray as black in it, and the lines on her forehead and beneath her eyes went deep. The laugh lines, not so much. They creased as she gave me a sympathetic look.

I couldn't take her seriously. I left and made my way down the alley and onto the street. The night air was crisp and cold—great for untangling thoughts.

Kit wouldn't let me untangle them though. She followed me. "You're in trouble. What can I do to help?"

I wanted to scream. *Where was this when we were growing up? Where was this two years ago when Caleb was murdered in front of my eyes and I was laid up in the hospital?* But my chest hurt at the mere thought of bringing up Caleb in her presence.

I went inside the motorhome and she came in behind me. I'm not sure why I didn't lock the door. I stepped past her to get to the fridge. She barely stood as high as my shoulders. I needed a beer, or better, whiskey, but all I had was water and energy drinks. I sighed and sat down at the kitchen table, avoiding Wolfe's gluey blood.

Startled at first, Kit took a towel off the counter, put it over the blood, and sat down. She didn't say anything. Just watched me. The shape of her face and the furrow of her brow stirred something in the recesses, but more than anything, she was a stranger. Her hands were steady, her eyes clear.

"How long have you been clean?" I asked.

She pulled a necklace out of her blouse. On the chain was a medallion engraved with a diamond shape surrounded by the words *Time Equals Miracles* and *Recovery Equals Life.* On top of the diamond was a Roman numeral one.

That's it, one year?

She must've seen it on my face, and said, "It's been hard, with… It's been hard."

No shit. I watched him die. The thoughts were cold. My body was steel. *She can't even say his name.*

Kit looked down, her cheeks flushing. It emphasized how unkind time had been to her. Except time wasn't the real culprit, was it? The thin, white scars and old, shallow pockmarks that dotted her face were from scratching at meth mites. It made my blood boil. The familiar twinge in my jaw told me I was grinding my teeth, so I bricked a wall around Mason the kid. That shit didn't matter anymore. Mason the adult needed to focus.

"You want to help?" I asked. "Tell me about the Redding Police Department."

"What about them? They're more or less the same as any other police, far as I know. You *are* innocent, right? What's the harm in turning yourself in?"

"I could die."

"That video was really scary. But that's just two agents. The Redding police are their own department. Or we can go to the sheriff."

What was this "we" shit? She was *not* a part of this. She had no idea what we were dealing with here. Not to mention that, push come to shove, county sheriffs and city PDs were subordinate to these agents. I didn't understand the California DOJ-Attorney General-Bureau of Investigation-whatever-the-fuck bureaucracy, but I knew state law enforcement trumped local.

"The only cop I trust is off fighting his own battles. It's too risky."

"You're not Epstein, sweetie."

"The man we're after, Marshall, has a lot of money and connections in low places." I pulled up my shirt and showed off the scars on my belly. There were nine of them. Her eyes were dinner plates.

"This was done in LAC by one of Marshall's connects. By the

man who killed your other son."

Kit blanched. She had no response to that.

Goddammit, I didn't want to bring him up. But maybe now she'd understand what I was up against.

Tum-tum-tum. It was the sound of Hallenbeck's rubber-tipped cane tapping the door.

"Come in," I said.

He stood across the table from us.

"We…don't have time for this."

"Fire Order Six," I said, putting it in terms I thought he'd appreciate. "'Be alert. Keep calm. Think clearly.' *Then* 'act decisively.'"

"'Order Three. Base all actions…on the current behavior of the fire.' What you saw on the news and what…that doctor had to say? That's smoke. *This*…is the fire."

He held out the burner to show the blinking dot of Curione's crew—our only shot at bringing down Marshall—moving down the map.

I glanced at Kit. Was she right? Quit while I'm behind and go to the police? Maybe Hallenbeck, decorated Marine and CalFire captain, could keep that from going sour.

"The police won't put a lot of stock in anything I have to say, but they would listen to you," I told him. "You're credible. You know I'm innocent."

"I didn't see…him shoot her."

"Are you fucking kidding me?" My heartbeat thundered in my ears. Yeah, it had happened fast, but who gives a shit that he didn't see *that* moment? He saw everything else *and* got shot at by these bastards.

"Talk about splitting hairs. You were there. You know I didn't kill her. I mean, you've said it yourself. I'm not a killer." Hallenbeck could tell the cops what he *did* see. Would it be enough to get me off the hook for Jasmine's murder? "If we get a statement from you *and* a statement from Wolfe…"

He rapped his cane on the ground to interrupt, but the words weren't ready.

"More…like…likely…they call me an accomplice." I'd had the same thought earlier today. He went on, "And you won't…get a statement from Sean without the safe."

Kit twisted the necklace in her fingers, watching us.

"Go to…the police now," he went on, "we're further back… than before. No evidence."

He was right. Again. Even *with* the safe full of incriminating evidence, Wolfe had been in hiding. And if I turned myself in, who would do the intake? The agents who wanted me dead? And if I survived turning myself in, Marshall could make sure I didn't survive jail. *And* he'd have our best chance of taking him down: the safe.

"We need…the safe back," Hallenbeck said. "If…if you don't see this through, you'll never live down what you've done. You have to see this through."

He was right, wasn't he? I rounded on Kit.

"We're taking the truck."

She looked at me, then at Hallenbeck, pursing her lips.

"All righty. But I'm coming with."

My jaw tightened. It was an effort to keep my teeth from grinding.

"You're not a part of this."

"You're the one who showed up in my garage. You made me a part of this."

I shot Hallenbeck a *She's gotta be kidding* look. He just tapped the phone: *They're getting farther away.*

Act decisively.

"Get your shit, Kit. We leave in five minutes."

"Bring your shotgun," Hallenbeck said.

She shook her head, face scrunched in disapproval.

"For self…defense," he added.

"Is it really self-defense if you're going looking for trouble?"

I'd thought the same thing about Hallenbeck's rifle when our trip first started, but now I was leaning toward his way of thinking. *I wonder what that says about me.*

"Five minutes," she confirmed, stepping out of the motorhome. "And if you leave without me, I'm calling the police."

"Congrats. You're both accomplices now," I grumbled as she hustled off back toward her place.

CHAPTER TWENTY-TWO

Nick Curione

-1730-
-END-TO-END ENCRYPTION ACTIVE-

NC: Wolfe was in McGreary, a town in Northern California. He wasn't lying about having an insurance policy. There's a safe, contents unknown. My team has possession. Do you want us to destroy its contents?

EM: No. I need to know what he has.

Curione nodded to himself. You can't clean up a mess you don't know about.

EM: No one opens it but me. Failure to comply is a capital offense.

NC: Understood.

Curione was not Marshall's first fixer, but he was determined to be the last. His first task upon obtaining the position had been to eliminate his predecessor.

The existing text glowed, no additional messages forthcoming. Curione's report wasn't finished. He took a breath and shut his eyes, glad Marshall couldn't see him.

NC: Less success with other targets. Jones brought in his former parole agent. That's taken care of, should work in our favor. Laid down heavy fire and it's possible one of them got hit, so we're canvassing regional hospitals and urgent cares, should know more soon.

EM: Wolfe is at Mercy Medical Center, Mt. Shasta.

Damn. Curione knew that Marshall had other sources, and incredible resources at his disposal, but he had gotten that intel damn quick. Had Wolfe been stupid enough to check in using his own name? A new message cut his astonishment short.

EM: And the others?

Very few things scared Curione. Telling Marshall this next part was one of them.

NC: Jones and Hallenbeck's location currently unknown.

EM: You lost Mason Jones?

I let a low-rent felon get the better of me, Curione thought. The disbelief he'd felt when it happened had turned to cold fury. He was determined to get leverage on Jones before engaging him again.

NC: Yes, sir.

Curione waited for the axe to fall. It was a full minute before Marshall replied.

EM: I'm returning stateside. No one opens the safe. Bring it to Redhorn and keep it SECURE.

CHAPTER TWENTY-THREE

FROM: ASAC, FBI FIELD OFFICE LOS ANGELES
TO: ADIC, FBI FIELD OFFICE SACRAMENTRO
SUBJECT: MCGREARY/DEL RIO INCIDENTS

At 10 pm, the sky was a charcoal awning and the ocean was a restless black vastness, turning silver where its waves lapped on Humboldt Beach. The dunes around the beach made their own frozen waves. The wind was bitter and there were only a few brave souls taking in the beauty.

"It's peaceful," Prescott said, slowing the sedan so they could scope out the waterfront. Luo arched an eyebrow at her, then took a shotgun out of the back seat. As if his service weapon wasn't sufficient. He needed to blast Jones apart.

The beach parking lot amidst the dunes had only a handful of vehicles in it. One of them was Jones' motorhome, and it was in the row closest to the beach.

"A hiding in plain sight thing?" Prescott wondered aloud, trying to engage Luo again. He'd said little since they found the image of the vehicle in the CALTRANS database, headed south on the 227. From the hospital, Prescott had gotten a pixilated surveillance cam image of the motorhome. She'd cross-checked that with DMV and DAPO files, and got the make, model, and license number. It was registered to Joshua Ortiz, Jones' buddy, and Jones had been living in it during his parole. Prescott and Luo had neglected to share their findings with the law enforcement community.

Luo did not respond to her question.

Prescott parked on the curb, using a bike rental hut to hide the sedan from the motorhome's line of sight. It was unmarked, but she didn't want their quarry to notice a fresh vehicle in the lot. She'd also been hoping Luo would cool down and start thinking straight. She'd hoped in vain. She didn't want Jones dead. She wanted him talking.

They got out and approached the motorhome, Luo with his shotgun at the low ready. The milky light from the crescent moon revealed dozens of tiny perforations on the motorhome.

"Bullet holes," she whispered, trying to get Luo to look at her. "There were bullet holes in the church too. Casings from multiple types of weapons. Indicative of an *exchange* of small arms fire. That sound like the cut-and-dry murder Sisk County is calling it?"

He shushed her and chambered a shell. The shotgun attracted the attention of an adventurous surfer wading into the rollers. A woman in neon activewear was roller skating down the bike path, saw them, and skidded to a stop.

Darn it, Prescott thought. She needed to talk him off the ledge.

"Cuffs and questions. Not bullets and blood," she said. She'd always had a flair for poetry.

Luo scoffed.

"So he can bullshit us? This guy impersonated a firefighter for multiple felony escapes from his hand crew. He's slippery as fuck," Luo said.

They reached the motorhome. A human shape was visible on the bed through the meshed window, its torso rising and falling in calm rhythm. Sleeping.

Prescott put her hand on her holster, getting ready.

"He might have some useful information," she hissed.

"Like his motive? It doesn't matter *why* she's gone." He was shaking.

"Like why he lured her *200 miles away* to kill her, when he could've done it in LA in a much smarter, cleaner way!" Prescott snapped. If she could make him curious—make him stop and *think*—maybe she could stop him from busting down the door and splattering Jones.

"There are people everywhere," she noted. *Witnesses.*

Luo slapped himself on one cheek, then the other. Psyching himself up.

"Police, put down your weapon!" he shouted.

Ah, I see what you did there, Prescott thought.

The shape on the bed stirred as Luo charged into the door shoulder first. It rattled, the panel cracking. He charged again, and a screw shot out of the bottom hinge. Luo charged a third time—Prescott yanked the shotgun, ripping it from his hands and spinning him—off balance, he busted through the door headfirst. She leapt over him and bounded up the deep door well.

The skunk of weed was what hit her first. It was overpowering. The sleeper leapt out of bed, hands up, wide-eyed and screaming, "Don't shoot!"

It wasn't Mason Jones. It was just some 20-something pothead.

Dazed and red-faced, Luo staggered up the steps with his service weapon drawn. He saw the terrified young man and stomped down the hallway of the motorhome, throwing the pistol on the floor. He glared at Prescott, then at the pothead, like it was his fault he wasn't Jones. Luo toppled the fridge, screaming in rage.

CHAPTER TWENTY-FOUR

A few hours earlier...

O ne hundred dollars?" I scoffed at Hallenbeck, dumbfounded. He sat in the passenger seat, and Kit was in the narrow backseat of the cab, watching the skyline: green ropes of orange groves set ablaze by a sinking sun.

He'd only gotten *100 dollars* for the motorhome.

"All I've done to fix it up, it's worth at least two thousand." Sure, it had some bullet holes in it, but it was a restored, vintage motorhome. "And it wasn't ours to sell!"

"Good trade..." He held up his finger to stop me interjecting. "The buyer is helping us out...confusing the trail."

I had a queasy feeling about what he meant. "How so?"

"Brought down...the price in exchange for him...driving it

far from Redding. Any...direction but south." The direction we were heading.

I goggled at him. The man was off his rocker.

"Aren't there agents out there who want to kill my son and think he's in that motorhome?" Kit asked, turning her attention inside.

Hallenbeck looked to me for support.

"What she said!"

Hallenbeck shrugged and watched the orange groves zing past. "That's...that's why it was 100 bucks."

I shivered. He'd wanted to beat Wolfe with a hammer. He'd wanted to leave him bleeding out at a truck stop. And now he was putting an innocent man in danger. That's why I didn't trust his heart. I knew it too well. The fire behind that cold line of thinking had a way of escaping containment.

"Careful, Mark," I warned. We needed to have a talk, but it'd have to wait until we could get some privacy.

Kit, the person preventing that privacy, shifted in the back seat.

To avoid questions and conversation, I turned on the radio, shuttling through country, Christian, and pop before I found an oldies station. That had to be the way to go with this crowd. The Supremes only got through one "*crying, baby for you*" and one "*sighing, baby for you*" when Kit cleared her throat. I hummed along and ignored her. She cleared her throat again. Louder. Sighing, I turned it down.

"So, where are these people taking the safe?" she asked.

"We don't...know," Hallenbeck replied.

"Yet," I added.

"All righty. And just, you know, for my edification, are these the people that killed your parole officer?" she asked.

"Yeah."

"And they want to kill you too?"

"If they got the chance, they would."

In the rearview, Kit twisted and untwisted the NA medallion, the chain cinching and loosening around her neck. "And your plan is to catch up and take the safe from them?"

"They don't know we're on their tail. We're in a different car. It's night. We can take them by surprise."

"All righty."

Kit went quiet for a spell. Then she leaned over the center console and eyed Hallenbeck.

"So, how'd you drag my son into this?" she asked.

"Going after Sean…was his idea."

"Which turned out to be right," I said.

"Sean is the man in the hospital?"

Hallenbeck nodded.

"Your son saved his life…"

"Macie!" she chirped, beaming.

Hundreds of times. That was how many times I'd told her I *hated* that nickname. She had to have been sober at least a few of those times.

"And fucked…everything up in the process," Hallenbeck added.

Kit *hmphed* and patted my arm. I edged away and focused on the tracker app. I didn't need her approval.

"We're still in the game," I said, pointing to the GPS dot. "We're actually gaining on 'em."

"Ideas...for if we catch 'em...on the road?"

"I'm thinking," I said.

I reached for the volume knob on the stereo.

"Mark? It is Mark, right?" Kit asked. Not done interfering, she stayed leaning over the console. Hallenbeck nodded in reply, and I left the knob alone. *Dammit.*

"What exactly is your role in this, Mark?"

Hallenbeck looked at her askance. It was obvious he wanted to respond the same way I did: "*What exactly is yours?*"

"I'm...the bank," he said.

"And yet you needed to steal my truck? That's curious."

"I'm curious...to see how your upholstery skills help...with all this."

Kit huffed, narrowing her eyes.

"There's probably more to it than that, right?" I chimed in, not even sure why I was coming to her defense. Maybe it was the *Only I can crap on my family* thing.

"I restore antiques and furniture and do custom woodwork. There's a lot of stripping, sanding, and refinishing, but there's also sourcing or creating hardware. Old brass handles and things..." Kit's face lit up with passion, "or making a replacement piece from new wood and figuring out how to make it match the existing item."

"So you kinda like it, huh?" I asked.

"I love it," she said.

"Kit the craftswoman." It was weird to think of her as a person and not a problem. I could grasp that in my brain. But in my bones? The wall I'd put up was there for a reason.

"It's good to have a craft," she added with a pointed look.

Subtle. She was the last person I needed career advice from. Is that what she saw her role as here, an advisor? Maybe it was her way of finally completing Step 9. But we were beyond amends. I drummed the wheel to a barely audible Motown song from the radio, missing half the beats.

At dusk, the highway had become a lava flow, anesthetic to my senses. I let it flow. She was here because she'd caught us. She was here so I could keep her from going to the authorities. Didn't care how sober she was now. The glass bitch had lost the right to give advice a long time ago.

"Hey, Mason," Hallenbeck barked.

"Hello?" That was Kit. She cleared her throat, bringing me out of hypnosis. Seemed they'd been trying to get my attention, and they pointed at the GPS tracking app.

The blinking dot was stationary now, in place just north of Sacramento.

"They stopped," I said, stating the obvious. "We're only a half-hour behind now."

Blue-black irrigated fields stretched on both sides of the highway, the night sky above brown and gray with light pollution. Ahead, Sacramento's glow turned the horizon into a mustardy haze. Hallenbeck had his rifle on his lap as we approached the real-world location of the blinking dot. Kit shrank below the bottom of the window, even though no one on

Curione's crew was expecting this vehicle or even knew who she was. Ominously, the dot hadn't moved since we first noticed it had stopped. We had caught up completely.

A chill trickled up my spine. *Ambush?* I exchanged glances with Hallenbeck, who had the same question in his eyes. He checked the chamber on his rifle. A round was loaded.

"They don't know we're in this truck," I reiterated. "Let's drive by and see what we see."

As we got closer, we saw Wolfe's rusty pickup on the embankment of the northbound lanes. After going hundreds of miles south. Interesting. The cabin looked empty and the bed definitely was.

We passed it from the southbound lanes with no surprises, so I turned around through the median and passed it again from the northbound lanes. It sat on gravel and patchy grass. No bushes nearby for shooters to hide in. Though someone could be crouched down in the cabin itself.

I parked a hundred yards away and turned off the headlights. It took my last ounce of self-control to sit still.

"Flashlight or no?"

"Better…not. Let your eyes…adjust," Hallenbeck said.

We sat in the darkness until our eyes were ready.

"Stay here and stay low," I told Kit.

Pale and frowning, she watched us step out. Hallenbeck held his rifle at the ready and I had a fresh stun gun. A brisk wind raised goosebumps on my arms. Or maybe it was nerves.

"Dispersion," he said, making a stuttering fan gesture. That must be Marine for spread out.

I did as he said. My eyes cut over the blocky darkness. The only movement was yellow-white reflections racing by in the windows of the truck. I didn't see anyone in it or under it. Hallenbeck's cheek was welded to the stock, his right eye was glued to the sights, but the muzzle bobbed unsteadily. What if this was the time he failed? What if this was the time he wasn't clutch?

We stalked to the vehicle with no incident. Hallenbeck circled to an angle on the driver-side door and nodded at me. I ripped it open. Nothing. Then the cab. No one. Then the truck bed— completely empty. The truck was abandoned. Just like us, they'd changed vehicles.

When Kit joined us, she claimed it was a sign to call it quits.

"You tried, Macie."

"Mason. *Mason.* Macie is a lady singer who made a cameo in my favorite *Spider-Man* movie. I am a man!"

"Okay. But your tracker thing is here and the bad people and the safe are gone."

She made it all sound so stupid and juvenile. I breathed deep, trying to calm myself, the tarry stink of rubber clouding my thoughts. Glaring headlights and whooshing cars interrupted the ones that broke free. The weight of a passing semi vibrated through the asphalt. My feet were heavy. My arms were heavy. My *ass* was heavy.

"Like you said, they changed cars," Kit continued. "This is Sacramento… They could've gone anywhere from here."

They could've. The capital was like the pelvis, with major arteries that branch into arterioles and then capillaries in the farthest reaches of California—hundreds of vessels pulsing to and fro.

But they'd ditched the car on a northbound embankment.

"It's 250 miles from McGreary to here. They went 250 miles *south* before they ditched this truck on the *northbound* 99. It's a misdirect. They're continuing south," I said, with more confidence than I felt. Kit frowned. Hallenbeck raised his eyebrows, intrigued. "And I think I know where they're headed."

CHAPTER TWENTY-FIVE

FROM: ASAC, FBI FIELD OFFICE LOS ANGELES
TO: ADIC, FBI FIELD OFFICE SACRAMENTRO
SUBJECT: MCGREARY/DEL RIO INCIDENTS

Rita Hallenbeck didn't let Prescott and Luo in the house. She stood in the crack of the door in a bathrobe and slippers with her brow deeply furrowed.

"Do I need to have a lawyer present for this conversation?" Rita asked.

The mistrust irked Prescott. Civilians didn't respect law enforcement in California. The whole state needed an attitude adjustment.

"We don't think your husband has done anything wrong," Prescott lied.

From the pothead, they'd learned about the man who'd sold

him the motorhome: Mason Jones' accomplice. The seller had weak hands, a cane, and talked slowly. Prescott had figured out that it was Mark Hallenbeck, a CalFire captain Jones had known from his time on an inmate hand crew.

"We think he's being taken advantage of," Prescott said.

Rita narrowed her eyes at that. "No one is taking advantage of my husband."

Luo grunted and hooked his thumbs in his pockets. Impatient.

"We're worried about his safety, ma'am," he said.

"He may not move as fast as he used to, but he can take care of himself."

"What if someone threatened you? Or your son?" Prescott asked. The Hallenbeck kid was away at SDSU, but it was plausible. "Could something like that make him do something out of character?"

All the walls Rita had put up crumbled.

And that was how they got access to Rita Hallenbeck's Find My Phone app. Mark's phone was off when they checked it, but it had last been powered on at a gas station in Pixley for a **Love you, all is well** text.

They were headed south on the 99.

Luo thought Jones was headed back to LA. Prescott thought differently.

CHAPTER TWENTY-SIX

Beneath a coal-black night sky, the lights of Del Rio's wineries made constellations across the hilltops. My brain was too spent to figure out what shapes they were. One of the stars in the constellation, Marshall's Redhorn Winery, glowed brighter and warmer as we approached. I turned off onto a campground called De La Uva in the nearby hills. *Of the Egg?* No, that wasn't right. Hallenbeck and Kit's heads lolled about as the suspension fought the bumps and divots of the dirt road. The high beams lit up scrub oak and acacia looming over us. I drove into the second-to-last campground before the road ended and parked.

I got out Burner #2.

Priority one: Ortiz. I shot a text to his burner to check in. He replied:

Safe. Holed up with fam in Castaic

I shut my eyes, muscles melting in relief. I almost fell asleep, but I flicked my earlobe and managed to reopen my eyes.

Priority two: I put my name in a search browser. My mugshot and a stack of headlines appeared instantly, then blurred. I blinked in an attempt to focus.

"You need to sleep," Kit said, leaning over the center console with bleary eyes.

"I'm not ready to call it a day yet," I muttered, hiding a yawn with my shoulder.

"It's tomorrow already."

I looked at the digits in the corner of the screen. 2:47 am. Shit. She was right.

I must've been exhausted, because I fell asleep with my head on the blaring words: *Manhunt underway for suspect in killing of parole agent.*

K amilah emerged from the crystalline water and smiled her dazzling smile. It was a sunny day, and we were in a lake surrounded by stately evergreens and snowcapped Cascades. Struggling to stay afloat, I churned water so I could stay locked on her radiant face.

Hallenbeck woke me up, swiping away a blanket either he or Kit had put over my head to block the sun now stabbing my eyes. One of them had also reclined the seat as far back as it went to make me more comfortable.

"Burning daylight," he said.

Crooked scrub oaks twisted around the campground like a fence, fracturing that daylight with crisscrossing shadows. Hallenbeck and Kit had sparked a crackling campfire and a small campground restroom cabin stood amidst the trees. There weren't nearly as many evergreens and there was a lot more chapparal. We weren't in the Cascades anymore.

My subconscious had plunked Kamilah and me in Lake Helen, and it reminded me that I'd been neglecting my notebook. I found my duffel bag behind the console and dug in, retrieving it. I flipped through the pages. It had very few scribbles dedicated to its original purpose, finding Wolfe. Instead, it had become my *After This* journal. If there *was* an "after this." *Should do an entry before I* really *wake up. Before I have to deal with reality.*

Underneath *Hike Lassen Peak (And Bumpass Hell? lol)* I added: *Lake Helen (swimming).*

I slid out of the truck, went to the restroom sink, and splashed icy water on my face. It was probably good there was no mirror. Stepping back out, I was surprised and irritated to see that Kit was still here. She was looking at her phone anxiously.

"Let me see that." I snatched the phone away.

A missed call from Frankie. And a bunch more missed calls from numbers that weren't programmed in as contacts.

"They're the police," Kit said. "A lot of them left me voicemails. And I just ignored them. That's the position you put me in. Ignoring the police."

"You wanted to come along."

All the same, I was being an asshole. She was under pressure and hadn't bailed. She was risking a lot to be here. If Curione's crew hadn't brought the safe to the Redhorn estate like I suspected, we were all completely fucked.

"Call your sponsee back. I don't want her to fall off the wagon. Then turn it off and put it in this, okay?"

I gave her a Faraday pocket.

"All righty."

"And she better keep her mouth shut about seeing us."

"I'll make sure," she said.

A twinge warbled up my back and every muscle in my body ached. Yesterday's activity was taking its toll. I trudged to the fire, and as I went through every stretch I knew, I watched Kit pace among the oaks on her phone. Her tone was urgent, her voice hushed, but I heard her say, "Please, Frankie," and listening to the reply, give a shaky, "Thank you."

Letting relief wash over me, I turned my thoughts to the mission. If the safe was on Marshall's Redhorn property like I thought, we needed to figure out where. I was betting it was on the commercial side of the property and not the residence. Close by but deniable, in case someone outside his circle were to notice it. There were all kinds of big boxes and equipment in a working vineyard. It'd be like hiding the safe in plain sight.

We also needed to locate it without getting noticed. I was wanted for murder, and thanks to Curione, both Hallenbeck and I were on Marshall's radar. Plus, his disability made him slower and more memorable. Unfortunately, we needed Kit.

After she turned off her phone and put it in the Faraday pocket, I nodded her and Hallenbeck over. *My accomplices,* I reflected, stomach flopping.

"Need help?" Kit asked.

"Yes. Not with my stretches." I explained how she could go to Redhorn Winery posing as a normal middle-aged woman trying some wine and taking in the sights, but instead of the Rio and the rolling hills around it, she'd be looking for signs of the enemy.

"I don't like this," Kit said.

"It was your choice to come along," I countered.

"I wanted to look out for you."

"You can literally do that by going and being a lookout for me."

She pursed her lips at that.

"I don't drink. I shouldn't even be around it. And you want me to pretend to be a winery customer."

"Maybe they…have non-alcoholic wine," Hallenbeck offered. "That stuff is…all the rage."

"Perfect. Ask about that," I said.

"If they don't?"

"It doesn't matter!" A dull throb pulsed in my temple. "It's a beautiful spot. Buy some cheese and take some goddamn pictures. All you have to do is find the likeliest places they'd hide a safe. Low-traffic areas, unused buildings. I think even you can handle it."

"Rude, Mason, rude," she *tsked*. "It's not a question of being able to—"

"This isn't a discussion, Mom." The throb turned to pounding, and I massaged my temple. I could feel cracks chinking in the wall. "Do it or go home."

I held out Burner #2 and waited.

Eyes glassy, Kit took it and left.

I drank beers with Hallenbeck to avoid looking myself up online. The drinks had been an essential purchase at the Pixley gas station. Less than 24 hours with Kit had turned me into a self-medicator. Fantastic. She came back an hour and a half later, too soon for my liking, and scowled at our beers.

"Can you put those away, please? It was bad enough up there."

I acquiesced, respectful of the addict.

I looked at the pictures she had taken. She'd been smart enough to disguise the intel-gathering pics as selfies, which was good. But there wasn't a single image with useful information. She'd stayed in the main tasting and restaurant area. I knew from my last visit that there was a barrel room where they gave tours, and much more that could've been explored.

It must've shown on my face.

"Sorry, I'm not much of a spy."

No shit. Looks like you didn't really try. Why was she even here? Looking out for me, my ass. Bubbling, volcanic heat threatened to surge through the cracks in the wall. I took a deep breath.

"Thanks. These are perfect," I told her.

She smiled and went back to the truck to unload a case of non-alcoholic wine.

I shot Hallenbeck a look. They weren't.

I looped on a surgical mask as Hallenbeck dropped me off at the Redhorn Winery welcome sign. I thought a baseball cap would be a step too far, that it would be too obvious I was trying to be incognito. More suspicious by trying to be less so. I did wear sunglasses though.

It didn't take me long to case the place. I took the tour, and a woman named Lisa took me and four couples through the crush pad and processing building, a barrel room, and to the tasting area. This tasting area was where Kit had snapped her useless selfies and it was where I'd cut myself on broken glass before all this began. Tour guide Lisa said this was the *new* tasting area—which meant there was an *old* tasting area. After the tour, I rescued myself from the trap of sipping wine with gabby Gabriela and her fiancé Ben to make my way off the beaten path.

I strode briskly around the large crush pad and processing building. The key thing in moments like this is to just pretend you belong. I was Pete McLean, professional vintner. What did vintners do? No idea.

At the edge of a sheer hill stood the old tasting area. There was no foot traffic over here. The building was a one-story with a decorative rock formation and concrete tables out front, and a creek running parallel to it. Probably my favorite thing about it was the *CAUTION: CONSTRUCTION* tape tacked around it and the *CLOSED FOR RENOVATION* sign.

In and of themselves, those warnings didn't mean anything. There was no construction happening here though. I stooped to examine the posts holding up the tape and the sign. The holes were pristine. No erosion from the wind wiggling the posts back and forth millimeters every day. Very recently placed. I went around back, throwing myself to the ground just in time.

A man stood at the back door. I crawled into the creek bed, which kept me below his eyeline as his gaze swept my way. He didn't see me. He wasn't wearing a uniform of any kind, but his demeanor and alertness screamed security. He wore a jacket despite the fact it was 70s and sunny. Probably concealing a weapon. Promising. I mucked through the muddy trickle that was the creek to get a better angle. There was a window to a breakroom with another guard, and this one didn't conceal his weapon. Two armed guards protecting a construction site with no visible construction materials or workers? And there was another promising detail on the back end of the building: a separate, gated access road that wound down the hill from it.

I kept low in the creek, ducking under a rustic wood bridge and heading back the way I'd come. Before the processing building blocked it from sight, I caught a sight that clinched it. Another man strode to the front entrance of the old tasting room, zipping up his fly. He had a long nose, a sloping forehead, and no chin. Ratface.

The building, the hillside, the river valley—everything snapped into sharp relief. The safe was here.

O kay. Who wants the safe?" I asked. Back at the campground, I paced around the ashes of the fire, bursting with buzzy energy. Hallenbeck and Kit sat listening.

"Is this a…pep talk? We do." Hallenbeck scratched his stubble, squinting at me.

"And Marshall does. That's what all this is about. He's the only one who wants it just as much as we do. He killed Boone to get his hands on it. To find out what evidence is inside, do whatever he has to do to cover his ass, and then destroy that evidence. There's a reason it's sitting in a building with armed guards protecting it when it could already have been opened and destroyed. Marshall isn't—"

"You didn't see the safe," Kit interrupted.

"Why else would armed guards be there? One of them is a guy who attacked us at Wolfe's church. Let me finish my thought."

Kit motioned for me to continue.

"There's a reason it hasn't already been opened and the evidence destroyed. Marshall isn't going to watch it get broken open on FaceTime and have a hired gun do a show and tell of what's inside. He's not going to trust even a lieutenant with this. These secrets could destroy him. He's going to be there in person."

"We don't know…for sure that…he'll do that *here*," Hallenbeck said.

"You're right. But Marshall is a busy executive with a detailed schedule and employees. It's time to go phishing."

"Umm…" Hallenbeck murmured.

"What?" Kit asked, face scrunching up.

"With a P-H," I explained.

"Right…"

"That was a lot cooler in my head," I said, cheeks and ears burning.

"Still my goofy one," Kit smiled.

I forced myself to return the smile, even though I was annoyed. She thought she really *knew* me? But I needed a friendly female caller for this gig. I needed dates and details. I needed her.

We prepped with some online research and then gave Kit a burner. After five calls to Redhorn Winery entities that went nowhere, she finally got connected to the head winemaker, Yvonne. She put it on speaker so all three of us could hear.

"This is Anabelle from the Blue Ridge Barrel Company," Kit began, adding a cringe-inducing country twang to her voice. Hallenbeck grimaced and shot me a look. I made a *bring it down a notch* motion to Kit. She glared at us as she continued, "I met Mr. Marshall a while back and he had an interest in trying out our oak barrels at Redhorn. My team is in California for a bit and I wanted to set up a meeting."

"Wonderful. I hope you enjoy your time here. I'm…hmm… I'm not aware of any meeting with the owner, and we're happy with our current supplier."

"I hear ya," Kit replied. "There's no harm in getting something scheduled, though, is there? Can always cancel if it's not what the boss wants. When will Mr. Marshall be on the Redhorn property?"

"Wish I could help, but I run the winery, not Mr. Marshall's schedule. And I'm surprised to hear he wanted a meeting," Yvonne said, her response choppy with doubt. "Unless he's hosting an event, he's pretty hands off."

"It's because we're the only company with access to lateleaf oak."

"Really?" Yvonne sounded intrigued. "Maybe we *should* have a meeting then. I believe Mr. Marshall is out of the country, but we could circle back when he returns."

"That would be great. Can you provide us the contact information for Mr. Marshall's assistant so we can coordinate this?"

"You don't have it?" The doubt crept back into the winemaker's voice.

Kit sighed dramatically. "I thought we did! But between you and me, our front-of-office needs some retraining."

Yvonne chuckled in understanding and provided the phone number for Marshall's assistant. I wrote it down in my notebook while the ladies exchanged thank yous and ended the call.

"That's a start," Kit said, eager for approval.

"Not bad," I admitted. "Is lateleaf oak a real thing?"

"It is. Very rare, even seemed like it was extinct for a while. Seemed like something a rich jerk would use for his wine barrels." Kit glared at Hallenbeck. "Guess my woodworking background came in handy after all."

"Did it?" He scowled. "Didn't…get much out of that."

"We got a number for his assistant," I said.

"And we know he's out of the country," Kit added.

"According…to that lady. Not very solid."

Kit ignored him and addressed me. "Is this Marshall's main home?"

"I have no idea. He has places all over the world."

"Hmm." She typed into the phone and studied the search results. Closing her eyes, she rolled her shoulders back and stood up straighter. Then she dialed the number I'd written down.

"Good afternoon, this is Margaret Baker from the Heritage Household Staffing Agency," she said in a prim British accent, and this one was jaw-droppingly spot on. Kit tapped my mouth closed with a smirk. "We have a service request for the Redhorn estate and we'd like to confirm the dates, please."

Along with my amazement came a watery feeling of kinship. *So this is where I got my talent for bullshit from.*

The assistant responded by typing into a keyboard, the tip-tapping coming rapid-fire over the line. Kit had the burner on speaker again.

"Heritage? I booked Colonial yesterday," the assistant replied. She didn't give her name and her tone bordered on hostile. But that wasn't what mattered.

I wrote *yesterday* in my notebook and showed it to my accomplices. They nodded in understanding. Yesterday was the day Curione attacked and acquired the safe.

"Who put in your request?" the assistant demanded.

"Quite strange, I shall see if I can track that down," Kit said. "In the meantime, what dates do you have, dear?"

Shall? Dear? I winced, and Hallenbeck shook his head. She was having a bit too much fun with this.

"I'm very busy and we already have a vendor."

Every word dripped with acid. It made me wonder what kind of people worked with Marshall on the legitimate side, and how much they knew about his illegitimate doings. Did he hire awful people, or did he turn them awful?

"Of course, we only want to make sure Mr. Marshall's needs are met," Kit said.

I tapped the word *yesterday* in my notebook and scribbled: *Get details.*

"I imagine some wires have gotten crossed with the last-minute changes," Kit ventured, taking a gamble.

"Probably someone from his security team. That's what happens when you cut a trip short without notice," the assistant fumed.

"I understand, dear."

"Sure. Colonial has the job and they're starting today, in fact.

Best regards."

The assistant hung up.

"*That's*…something!" Hallenbeck said. "Marshall…is coming here."

"Yeah, and soon," I said. "We can take that to the bank." We wouldn't be able to get a specific time without raising any flags, but soon *was* something. His household staff had been activated *today*, which meant Marshall would be at his Redhorn estate in a matter of days. The urgent tug in my gut was briefly overshadowed by admiration.

"Meryl Streep over here! Where did that come from?" I couldn't help but smile, and even Hallenbeck allowed a grudging smirk.

Kit blushed, beaming. "As it happens, I was onstage as Wendy Darling in a Peter Pan adaptation that was quite well received in the *Fresno Bee*," she said, still in the accent.

"Mm, quite. I daresay."

"Indeed." She went back to her normal voice. "I was 11 years old at the time, so *really*," she continued sheepishly, "I've kept up with the accent thanks to the *Great British Baking* show."

"Well, it worked great."

I clapped for her, and Kit took a bow. My chest felt lighter. She wasn't stealing my mowing money anymore. Ancient cinders crunched beneath my shoes as I stood and stretched. The wind met the ashy scent with fresh, green smells. I was invigorated.

Marshall had cut an overseas trip short and was coming to Redhorn within days. Multiple gunmen, including Ratface from Curione's crew, were guarding a building on the property. That meant I was right. The safe was here, and they were keeping it secure until he arrived to open it.

Finally, a break. This was my chance.

CHAPTER TWENTY-SEVEN

So, what now? We call the police and have them catch him in the act of opening it up?" Kit asked. The "we" part didn't bother me as much now.

"No," I said. "Too much could go wrong. Why would the police believe us?"

"What about an anonymous tip?"

"They're not going to bust into a winery and seize a random safe over a tip. If for some reason they actually took the tip seriously, which I doubt, they'd have to get a warrant, and by then Marshall would probably have opened it already."

Kit expelled a long, frustrated breath. "But we have to get the police involved, don't we? What's the point of all this, if not to prove to the authorities that Marshall is the bad guy here and you're innocent?"

"You're right," I said.

She perked up at that.

"That's why we steal the safe ourselves before Marshall gets here. Once we have it, we hide it and contact the authorities for a negotiated surrender. That's how I turn myself in and keep you both clean. With leverage. Having the safe in our pocket protects us."

"Let's…do it," Hallenbeck said, smiling grimly.

"Mason, you are really testing my sobriety today." She dug her fingers into her hair and paced. "I *am* here to help, but bending the law is one thing. Breaking it…" She shook her head.

"If you think…about it, we're…giving the law a little… unconventional help."

"Classic self-delusion. And I would know."

"I have a plan," I said.

Kit stopped pacing and crossed her arms. Hallenbeck watched me with keen interest. Using a charred stick and rocks to diagram the tasting room on the ground, I explained the plan. It was a really good one, from a guy who had gotten away with stealing a lot of shit. The peanut gallery had critiques though.

"Relies…too much on speed," Hallenbeck said.

"That's what makes it a smash and grab," I replied.

"Still," he said, and gestured theatrically at his cane.

"That's why most of it is on me," I countered.

"Relies too much on you then," he said, in a rare rapid-fire verbalization.

Temperature rising, I held back a snippy retort and shrugged.

"I caught you stealing my car," Kit said. "It wasn't Frankie with her young ears who heard it, it was my old butt. And now you think it's a good idea to try again with people who tried to kill you."

"Was that a question? Or do you just want me to feel like shit?"

I sounded like a baby, but fuck if that didn't hit a nerve. I used to steal cars for a living, got caught by my own mom, and now she was calling me out on it.

"I'm just being honest. Sorry if I don't want to see you get shot."

"Then contribute. I'm not hearing ideas from either of you, just naysaying."

Kit stormed off, saying she needed air. We were in the great outdoors with some of the freshest air possible, but I wasn't going to quibble with her.

"I have…some tweaks," Hallenbeck said.

"About time, Marine," I said.

Hallenbeck glowered but proceeded to tell me in his halting manner.

They were damn good tweaks.

We left Kit at the campground and headed into town to buy a hand truck (to move the safe quickly) and other key supplies. Thanks to something called Pioneer Day, a drive that should've taken ten minutes took forty. We had to turn around at three different street closure signs because of the *PARADE ROUTE.*

Past the signs and barricades were curbs lined with people, and over their heads, I saw a sparkly red, white, and blue float followed by a bright green tractor. Tractors? Pretty sure the pioneers didn't have tractors. As Hallenbeck watched the parade, I realized we finally had the privacy I'd wanted. The thought of him glaring at me with his ring of fire eyes turned my guts into a writhing mass, and I found myself unable to speak.

When we'd looped around the entire downtown, we made it to a sporting goods store just off Main Street. Just down the block, happy families crowded the curbs as floats and…a giant bull, I realized belatedly, passed by. Hallenbeck dropped me off, driving on to find a store with the chemicals, containers, and other *accoutrements* we needed.

Even wearing a surgical mask, it wasn't ideal for me to be out. Scouting the winery was bad enough, but it had to be done. We had a lot of stuff to buy. Kit was useless, and it was too much to put entirely on Hallenbeck's shoulders. Literally.

I hoisted a leg on the cart corral, trying to stretch the stiffness out of it. The thing was, I couldn't be around the birthgiver right now. She'd probably try to talk me out of all this. Feeling a smidge of relief in the muscles and joints, I switched legs. As I did, movement in my peripherals sent a jolt of dread through my chest.

Marching toward me was an Asian man and a white woman. The man had short hair and wore a dark green polo and tactical boots. The woman wore a blue polo, tennis shoes, and had her hair in a bun. Both had holstered pistols. From the look on his face, I knew the Asian man recognized me. From the way his jaw clenched and his eyes narrowed, I knew he hated me. These two were the agents the Good Doctor had warned me about. Luo and Prescott.

Luo's hand shot down to his holster.

"Put your hands up!" Prescott shouted.

I bolted down the street and turned a corner. *Shit. Shit.* How did they find me?

Maybe I could get lost in the crush of paradegoers. Turning the corner into the parade route, I was surrounded by families packed up to the curb. Heart battering my ribcage, I slowed to a casual walk and knelt by some kids, eyes on the parade. *Breathe. Breathe normal.* You're just a dude in the crowd. A dude focused on his peripheral vision. I hoped the two agents would run right past.

I hammered out a rapid-fire text from my burner to Hallenbeck's.

Seen by agents. Evading.

I concentrated on what I could hear. An overlapping hubbub of multiple engines. Tractors rolling down the parade route. People cheering. Hooves clopping. The thundering beats and trumpeting brass of an approaching marching band.

Rubber clomping—boot steps coming in fast—my pursuers. I wished I had the cowboy hat the old dude next to me was wearing.

"Move," a brusque male voice ordered. The Asian agent, Luo.

"Is everything okay, Officers?" a woman asked. They must've shown the bystanders their IDs.

"We're looking for a white male with dark hair and a tattoo on his hand," answered a crisp female voice. Prescott.

A prickle whisked up my neck. Were they looking at me? Scrapes and shuffling of feet—people stepping away from me. Clearing a path. Was someone pointing me out? The clashing cymbals and thudding drumline got closer, drowning out softer sounds. It was hard to tell, but I thought the voices around me got quieter. The movements of the people more cautious.

"Mommy?" a boy behind me cried out.

I shifted my head a smidge and cut my eyes in the direction I'd come.

A figure in dark green, stalking forward.

I ran into the parade, juking around a tractor, and sprinted at the marching band.

"Stop!" Luo shouted.

How to lose them? Tractors, horses, vats of baked beans—there were plenty of options for chaos. But…throw a band member's horn into the spokes of a tractor and the tractor could throw the driver. Slap the hindquarters of a horse and the horse could crash its wagon into the crowd. Tip over a vat of baked beans and the exposed burner scorches the cook or starts a fire. There was no distraction or disruption I could cause without hurting someone.

Steam from the vats and yelling and rippling colors and glinting brass—a gorgeous horse—and synchronized-uniformed steps and clamoring voices and trumpets. Overwhelming. Time to get out of the parade. Calves burning, a side stitch stabbing under my ribs, I pivoted from the confusion, toward the curb—

Pop pop! My heart skipped a beat—two gunshots—I ducked and spun around—Luo, his face a mask of rage, had his pistol pointed at the air.

"That's your warning. Stop running!"

Startled by the gunshots, a horse spun and neighed, its cowgirl rider flopping in and out of the saddle. This guy didn't give a shit about the collateral.

I sprinted for the cowgirl as she yanked the reins and dug her heels, but the wild-eyed horse bucked hard and she flew backward—

She knocked me to my knees, but I caught her.

"Oh my God," she gasped, in a daze.

I deposited her on the curb as the horse sprang off, hooves flying, families scattering. Breaths coming rapid and ragged, I hurtled into the crowd on the opposite side of the street. Jeering parents and confused kids pulling away—good—as I got through the curbside mass, sighted an alley, and put all my energy into my legs—

My Adam's apple flared and stars exploded—I smacked the ground on my back, head thunking concrete.

Two identical blurs loomed over me, swimming in a blue fog.

"Call it a day, buddy," they said, but with only one voice.

I squinted and they became one man. A thickset man, in jeans, a t-shirt, and a coyote brown baseball cap with an American flag on it.

"He's down," he shouted.

I tottered up and fell back down, cobwebs spreading over my vision. He put a tan combat boot on my chest. A hot storm of pain radiated from the back of my skull.

"Stay down," he said. Calm, but clearly not fucking around.

I just had to get clotheslined by a damn war vet.

"I got him," he said.

I pushed off the ground and threw my body up, back wrenching, off balance—the veteran stumbled back and grabbed a lamp post—I fell into a storefront window, fracturing the glass.

Chnk!

A bullet hole splintered the glass by my elbow. In shock, I saw Luo twenty yards away, his weapon horizontal this time and aimed at me. Onlookers screamed and scattered. My limbs went cold.

"Holster your weapon!" Prescott shouted.

Fwrunch. A stagecoach flipped, dumping hay bales that a float crashed into, and the agents stopped to help the sultry saloon girls tottering on it.

Rage leads to chaos. I knew that better than most.

The veteran charged, smashing me through the glass, and hardwood floor hit me like a Mack truck. Red agony blasted from my back and side—glass shards carving me up as he expertly twisted me around, wrenching my arm behind me until my shoulder screamed. His knee was on my back.

This was not the time for deep thoughts.

"Stay down!" he snapped.

I grasped a shard of glass with my free hand. It was a perfect shiv. I could slash the knee in my back…and end up cutting a ligament or even his femoral. I let go of the shard. The room around us was filled with bookshelves, but there wasn't a single book in reach.

"C'mon, man, this has nothing to do with you," I grunted.

"Put your other hand behind you," he said, yanking my arm back. I gasped, lightning lancing from my shoulder. He was going to rip it out of the socket.

I did. He was in control.

Rage leads to chaos.

What were the triggers Hallenbeck had said he hated? It was a long shot and a dick move, but…

"Thanks for your service, you fucking baby killer," I said.

"Shut the fuck up," he snapped, his knuckles thudding into the back of my head twice, three times—splitting my vision, wracking my skull with pain—but he no longer had control…and I wriggled and bucked him off.

Staggering to the back door of the bookstore, I toppled a bookcase to block the way behind me and careened into the back alley, head throbbing, stinging from cuts all over my body.

Walking purposefully, I took back alleys and side streets all the way to the outskirts of town, keeping an eye out for nosy bystanders and traffic cams. I didn't notice anything to cause alarm. No helicopter, no strobing blues and reds. It seemed the CDOJ agents were squelching a bigger search. That was an advantage, even though the reason was that they wanted me dead instead of captured. My hot, prickly upper body grated against my bloody, holey shirt as I went. My breaths ground in and out, scratchy as sandpaper. My Adam's apple was swollen and sore, and if I swallowed, sharp pain shot up my throat. I'd have to keep an eye on that. Swelling in the airway isn't great.

I stayed off the highway and walked through a vineyard toward the campground, which was nine miles away. The stench of cow shit hammered my nostrils. From what I could see, the grapes had been harvested, leaving only green leaves and fertilizer at the base of the vines. Why did they fertilize them *after* the harvest? Maybe they needed to recover from their grapes being taken. As I plucked a sliver of glass from my forearm, I wondered if the vines felt it. Like I felt the burning sting in the four-inch, jagged slice the sliver left behind. That was gonna need stitches.

My elbows twanged something fierce. Lucky for my brain, they'd taken a portion of the impact when I got clotheslined. *Lucky?* If I was lucky, I wouldn't have gotten clotheslined by a misguided do-gooder. I fingered the tender lump on the back of my head where I'd hit the concrete. My skull was still a throbbing mass of pain. Wasn't nauseous and didn't need to vomit though. My vision was clear. No concussion.

I read a text on my burner that Hallenbeck had sent some time ago, in response to my message about the agents.

Good luck. Will complete shopping.

I texted him my location. A half-hour later, he picked me up on a back road between vineyards. His eyes traveled over the scatterplot of cuts on my body.

"Damn. You…all right?"

"I'll be fine." It hurt to talk, and my voice came out as a quiet rasp.

"Followed?"

I shook my head and took a list out of my pocket. The words were distorted by crinkles, sweat, and a spot of blood on the word *hand truck*.

"Wasn't able to get my stuff," I croaked.

"Handled it. Every…thing from…both lists." He gestured behind us. In the truck bed, loaded plastic bags whipped in the wind. A few of them had the name of a sporting goods store on them—a different store than the one I'd been spotted at—and in the middle of it all was the hand truck.

"From memory?" I smiled, and it made my face hurt.

"Steel trap," Hallenbeck replied, struggling to make a head-tap gesture. He returned my smile, but it didn't reach his eyes. Something was wrong.

"What?"

He shook his head and kept his eyes on the road.

"Lay…later."

"Tell me."

He sighed and handed me Burner #4, with the screen unlocked and the messaging app open. There was a text on the screen. How did he have texts on it? The only person who should have the number was Ortiz, unless…

"Did you set up text forwarding?" I asked, making my throat raw. I wanted to shout, but that would *really* hurt.

Hallenbeck gave me a sheepish look.

"I have a…wife and kid."

He had signed into his cloud account and had his personal texts forwarded to a burner phone. That defeated the purpose of having a burner phone. Muttering a string of every obscene word I knew, I read the message.

This is the doctor from Mercy Medical. The patient you brought in died while I was off shift. Heart failure. Was stable and had good vitals before I left. I'm concerned about foul play. Wanted to inform. I'm sorry.

It sucked the air from my chest.

Wolfe was dead.

CHAPTER TWENTY-EIGHT

I understood the words, but I didn't want to believe them. I ran toward gunmen for him. Bandaged his wounds and took him to the hospital. And it was all for nothing. He'd died anyway. Not just died. *Been killed.* Chest constricting, I had to remind myself to breathe.

He hadn't been my friend, but he wasn't an enemy anymore either. I'd found him and earned his trust and brought him back from the Dark Side. He'd helped the Good Doctor warn us about Luo and Prescott. She was "concerned" it was foul play. I was 100% sure it was foul play. Marshall's people had gotten to him. *Because* I found him. *Because* I earned his trust.

Should I have left him in hiding?

My brother Caleb had tried to help someone who couldn't help himself, a young inmate named Andre, and was murdered for it. Was that the curse of the Jones boys? Do right and people die?

A wave of fatigue hit me, and it cut to the bone. I wanted to pass out in the passenger seat, but we had work to do. As soon as we got back, I needed to clean up and prep the gear for our smash and grab. I had to make all this mean something.

"We need to get that safe," I said.

"We do," Hallenbeck agreed.

I texted the Good Doctor back:

Don't share those concerns. It's the only way to protect yourself.

At a stop sign, Hallenbeck struggled to clap my shoulder, the Tin Man without oil. His arm slipped back, fingers curling of their own accord. I knew it was because of the damage to his central nervous system, but it still sent a chill down my spine.

When we got to the campground, I wove around a wide-eyed Kit and filled a bucket with soapy water from the campground bathroom. I peeled off my shirt and a piece of glass clinked onto the floor. The cuts wrapped around me, from my chest and stomach to my back. The skin was a deep pink, inflamed, and slick with sweat and blood. Without a mirror, I'd have to clean the back cuts by feel. Outside, Kit cleared her throat, and without waiting for a response, strode in. She looked me up and down and shook her head.

"Mason Alexander Jones, what have you *done* to yourself? Stop what you're doing and sit down by the fire," she said. "I'll get some antiseptic and take care of everything."

As if, I thought, and realized that not only were my walls crumbling, I was also becoming a 90s-era teenage girl. The throbbing in my skull intensified. It was like an invisible hand had taken to squeezing my brain like a stress ball.

"Why are you even here? *Really?*" I croaked.

"To help, sweetie."

"If you wanna help, find me a needle and thread," I said, my raspy voice cracking. "And don't drag your feet like you have with every other fucking thing."

She crossed her arms. "Since when can you sew?"

"Since prison."

"Don't be snippy. I have a sewing kit, and I'll see if there's some peroxide or rubbing alcohol around here too."

"That damages the skin. Soap and water is better."

"And since when are you an expert on wound care?"

"Since hand crew training and getting EMT certified." I didn't mention that I'd used my EMT training a total of one time before now, on Wolfe, and that in the end, it hadn't even mattered.

Kit pursed her lips, went outside, and came back with a needle and thread. She took my elbow and I allowed her to lead me to the cold firepit. I sat on a log and she got started with a clean washcloth and the soapy water. Hallenbeck shuffled over and set his first aid kit between us, Kit glaring at him as he did. Avoiding her eyes, I stifled a growl as the cloth scraped over the burning arroyos on my abdomen.

"You think that if you show the world Marshall is bad, that proves you're good," she said. It wasn't a question.

I bit back a *Not exactly*, because it was that exactly. She was pretty perceptive without the drugs. I hated it.

"Mark…" I began, "do you mind ops-checking the gas masks and night vision?"

Taking the hint, Hallenbeck went back to the truck bed, out of earshot, and started sorting through the new gear.

The ashes of the campfire stirred in a breeze. "I have a lot to make up for," I said.

"I can relate."

I fucking bet.

And yet I was glad she was here. Her face seemed softer, the scars on it fainter. She was being a mom. My headache faded to a dull pulsing.

"Have you really thought this through? From where I stand, I mean…" She hesitated. "You may not be an addict, but you got some kind of monkey on your back."

"It's called motivation. I'm motivated."

"However you feel…or *I* feel about the road I was on…" she struggled to find the words, "well, let's just say there's a lot of baggage that comes with that road and leave it at that. But I also learned some things. Is it so hard to believe I have some wisdom to offer?"

When it comes to exposing the man behind the destruction of thousands of homes, the man responsible for dozens of deaths? *Yeah, it is hard to believe*, I thought. She didn't have any skin in the game.

Not enough skin.

I kept quiet, scratching at dried blood—Wolfe's—on the first aid kit's fabric shell. Bits flaked off, but most of it got pushed in deeper.

I saw her face change. Her chin trembled and her gaze went distant.

"What happened to Caleb…" she began.

Don't.

"Was it really over contraband trafficking?"

"Jesus Christ, you wanna do this right now?" Raw cuts all over my body, a monstrous weight pressing down on me, and she wanted to open that wound?

"If not now, when? When are we going to have a real conversation, Mason?"

"I don't see the point."

I gasped as a sting shot up my back. Biting her lip, she showed me a two-inch long shard she'd pulled out.

"Shit," I said. "Do I need stitches back there?"

"I don't think so. Bandages for sure though."

She washed and wiped in silence. No more questions or commentary.

Maybe it was because of how small she was next to me. Maybe it was that she was trying to take care of me.

"Contraband trafficking, yes and no," I said. "He was killed because he was smuggling food to an extortion victim."

He was killed for doing the right thing, I thought. Maybe I was going to follow in his footsteps, but what else could I do? Ignore all the wrong I've done, the pain I've caused? Hallenbeck, the living reminder of my sins, stood by the truck bed, scrutinizing the seal of one of our new gas masks.

Not enough skin.

"And what does this man Marshall have to do with Caleb?"

"Nothing. But Grayson Graham, the man who murdered Caleb, is the kind of guy that Marshall hires. Real bad people."

"I see. Thank you."

Kit scrubbed the jagged cut on my forearm.

"Will you stitch that for me?" I asked. My hands were shaking from fading adrenaline.

"Of course."

She sterilized the needle with a match and pierced my skin, one more sting among dozens of others, but still, I winced. Maybe because I could see it. Her hands were steady as she ran the thread out and through, out and through, cinching the wound shut.

"All righty. Your turn," she said.

"What?"

"I'm sure you have questions too. Ask me something."

I checked to make sure my ass was still on the log and my feet were still on the ground, because the world had gone off-kilter. What a thing to say. It was beyond surreal to think about an honest exchange with her. Question after question surfaced in my mind, but they all funneled into one: Why couldn't you quit when it mattered? *Caleb and I were adults when you got clean.* Way too fucking late. And then Caleb was gone. Acid thoughts turning my stomach sour, I fought to keep my voice flat as I looked into her eyes.

"Why didn't you come see me when I was in the hospital?"

Kit finished the stitches and snipped the thread. She looked down.

"When I found out about Caleb…it was…it was bad, Macie. I was…" She sighed and didn't finish the thought. "I let the disease win," she said.

"Cancer is a disease, Mom. You not having the willpower to lay off the crank isn't a disease." I knocked the first aid kit into the ashes, blood burning hotter than my flayed skin.

There was no surprise on her face, but her lip trembled.

"Your 'disease' kept you from being a mom," I said. "You were all we had."

Her eyes got glassy. *Who gives a shit.*

"Once we were *gone* you got clean. And when Caleb was murdered *right in front of me* and I was laid up in the hospital, ope, your old disease took you out of the picture again. Disease, my ass! You were sad and gave in to drugs instead of seeing your only remaining son. *I* was sad too, and I looked for a way out. I almost killed myself. *I* own that. *I* did that. Not some 'disease.'"

She was racked by sobs now, tears flowing freely down her cheeks.

"I wasn't there when you needed me. More times than either of us can count." She sniffled and wiped her nose with her sleeve. "I'd tell you I was sorry if you'd accept it, but…sometimes you can't make amends. The people you hurt still got hurt. The glass gets stuck in a wound like that."

"It does." I stood and toweled off. Walls going back up, I fished the first aid kit out of the firepit and rummaged for the antibacterial gel. Kit wiped her eyes.

"Did Mark tell you the new plan?" I asked, smearing the gel on the cuts I could reach.

Kit reached out to help, then pulled back. She nodded.

"It's a three-person job. I need to know if you're in or out."

"I'm still here, aren't I?"

There was that.

"Why don't you set up a tent and get some rest? I'll wake you up when it's time."

Kit nodded again and took a tent bag.

I rattled ibuprofen tablets straight out of the canister and into my mouth, immediately regretting it as I gagged on the bitter, chalky paste it became. Eyes blazing over the campsite, I found a stale, unfinished beer to wash it down. I would never understand how people in movies just raw-dogged pills like that.

Finally had an explanation from her and it didn't mean shit. A predictable fucking explanation at that. And yet she was here. She was going to help. And that *did* mean shit.

I joined Hallenbeck against the truck bed and began the preparation of a bevy of water bottles and glass jars. My little surprises for the gunmen on the hill. Then I inspected the other additions Hallenbeck had bought while I was getting chased through a parade. When I was done, I double-checked, triple-checked, then quadruple-checked that everything was ready. Head, throat, and cuts still throbbing, I found that Kit had set up the second tent as well, laid down in it, and set an alarm for 1:45 am.

I don't remember falling asleep, but I woke to the sounds of hushed voices. Night had fallen and the only other sound was the rustle of leaves. It was only 8:12, still plenty of time until the job. I sat up, ignoring my achy everything to listen. It was Kit and Hallenbeck, arguing in the other tent. Though it was hard to hear what they were saying, I bet she was trying to see if he would quit. Fat chance. Their voices got angrier.

Mommy and Daddy are fighting.

I used my hand to muffle the sound of the zipper and crept out, sidling up to the other tent.

"Even if it kills him?" Kit hissed.

"He's a gur...grown man. He can make...his own decisions. He's done pretty damn well so far."

It was a deeply pleasant surprise to hear that from Hallenbeck. Despite everything, I *had* done well. Standing taller, I went back to my tent. If I was going to pull off a smash and grab with a TBI victim and a recovering addict, I'd need some rest.

CHAPTER TWENTY-NINE

FROM: ASAC, FBI FIELD OFFICE LOS ANGELES
TO: ADIC, FBI FIELD OFFICE SACRAMENTRO
SUBJECT: MCGREARY/DEL RIO INCIDENTS

The motel room stank of mildew. It was almost as bad as Wolfe's church. Prescott considered turning on the TV to see what the news was saying but decided against it. She needed to do something productive. Using the flashlight on her phone, she inspected under the comforter, sheets, and pillows. She checked under the mattress and behind the headboard. No bedbugs that she could see. Not that she planned on sleeping any time soon. Out of things to do, she resigned herself to checking on Luo and knocked on the door.

The sound of the shower continued from the adjoining room. It had been running for 30 minutes. *Leave some for the farmers,*

Kevin.

"You can't be still showering in there," she called.

He opened the door and went back to a rumpled spot on the bed. He was in shorts and tank top, his shower long finished.

"What the hell is wrong with me?" he asked, lying down to stare at the ceiling.

"Obsession is quite a cocktail," Prescott said. She went to the bathroom and turned off the shower.

"I was using that for white noise."

"It's wasteful."

"I haven't been listening to you," he muttered, clearly not referring to the water.

You don't say, she thought.

The aftermath of the chase had shaken Luo. It hadn't been the Del Rio PD sergeant's questions or his skeptically cocked eyebrows as he asked them. Luo had stared at his handiwork like a man released from a spell. Which wasn't far off. He'd gawked at the bullet holes in the bookstore, the cowgirl being interviewed by a uniform, the saloon girl getting a cut stitched by an EMT.

Their exchange with DRPD had been brief and redacted-on-the-fly. They'd vamoosed immediately afterward. If they weren't CDOJ special agents, they'd have been there all day.

"Why don't you let me take it from here?" she asked him.

"No." He sat up, shaking his head. "Leave you without backup? Over something *I* started? I can't do that."

"I hear what you're saying," she responded. *You'd be doing everyone a favor,* she thought. "Can you at least promise me bracelets instead of bullets? We need to be able to *question* Jones." Prescott hoped it was the last time she'd have to reiterate the concept.

A storm of emotions fought across Luo's face. He didn't answer.

She thought about how they had found Jones before and how they might again. Upon arriving in Del Rio, she had doubted that Jones and Hallenbeck would check into lodging. Even with fake identification, the risk of being noticed and remembered was too great. She thought they would camp instead. The problem was, there were 11 campgrounds in the Del Rio area, with who knows how many spots each. Jones didn't have the motorhome anymore, though, and would need camping gear. Del Rio only had *three* sporting goods stores—a much more manageable search grid. Luo had been skeptical, but her instincts had proven right.

Now, though, searching the campgrounds was the best option. She'd start with those closest to Marshall's property.

Luo drove his fists into the bed and shut his bleary eyes. He still hadn't answered her question.

"Kevin? Can you promise me that?"

CHAPTER THIRTY

The ringing alarm irritated me into wakefulness. *Need more sleep.* As my brain turned on and I remembered the mission, I dismissed the urge. 1:45 am. It was time. Hallenbeck was in the tent with me, and he was already awake.

"You've been wheeze…wheezing up a storm."

Such a thing is bound to happen when a war vet knocks you on your ass via your throat. My entire body was tight and aching. I climbed out of the tent and took my time stretching and downing the contents of a water bottle. Hallenbeck turned on a portable lamp, dazzling my eyes.

I went to Kit's tent and scratched the polyester, making a zippy sound.

"Knock knock," I said.

There was no response. There was no sound of a person stirring inside either.

I opened the tent and the lamplight spilled in. The tent was empty.

Hallenbeck cleared his throat.

Twisting the empty water bottle in my hands, I felt the plastic reach its limits, ripping and popping. I saw her lying in bed, tugging the cover over her eyes while I sweated and vomited. "*Not now, Macie.*" I threw the bottle in the tent and repressed a shout. Chest aching for reasons that had nothing to do with yesterday's ruckus, I took a moment to compose myself before turning to Hallenbeck.

"Desertion," he said. He held something at his side. It looked like a bandage wrapper.

"Yeah." What else was there to say?

Of course she'd left. Things had gotten hard.

I scoured the tent. The Faraday pocket that had held her phone was empty. She'd been with us for a day and some change, and I had a firm hope that there wasn't yet a warrant to track her phone. My hope that she wouldn't call the cops herself was more fragile.

"Let me see that."

Hallenbeck held onto the bandage wrapper for a moment, then shrugged.

There was a handwritten note scribbled on it. Two sentences in Kit's curvy, feminine scrawl.

He doesn't have your best interests at heart. Neither do you.

I didn't expect her to understand. She hadn't been through what Hallenbeck and I had. *Not now, Macie.* Of course she'd left.

Of fucking course. I crumpled up the note and tossed it in the cold firepit.

He adjusted his grip on his cane and looked up at the stars. It was a clear night.

"No…offense, but it's not…a big loss," he said.

She must've called a taxi or ride share, because her truck was still here. Logistically speaking, he was right. And non-logistically speaking, maybe she was too. Hallenbeck was dead set on the mission, and not because he cared about my past or future. It was because he was pissed and had something to prove. But he was the one who was here. Seeing this through with me, no matter what.

"Even if it kills him?" she'd asked.

It wasn't getting killed I was afraid of. It was getting killed before I could make up for all the wrong I'd done. If I died, the authorities would never get the evidence in the safe. Without it, they'd have no reason to protect Hallenbeck from Marshall's hitmen. I might not make it, it was true. By the police or Marshalls' crew, I might get gunned down like Boone—but not before I tried to fix this. Unlike Kit, I wasn't going to abandon my responsibilities. My sins.

"Well?" Hallenbeck said, interrupting my thoughts.

"Deserters gonna desert," I shrugged.

"Need…a third."

"Yup," I said.

I did the only thing I could. Something I hated with every fiber of my being. I'd wanted him clear of all this.

I called Ortiz.

"Trust, this better be an emergency," he groaned over the line.

"How fast can you get to Del Rio?" I asked.

I n position on the hillside of the winery, we waited. Echoing from the surrounding rises, jabbering woofs and plaintive shrieks joined with high-pitched ululating howls. I knew it was only coyotes, but the howls reminded me of sirens. The echoes made it impossible to pinpoint where the coyotes were, and it was good to know that we'd have the same advantage when making noise on the hilltop above.

At 3:52 am, Ortiz materialized out of the darkness. His swagger had 50% less pep than usual, and the creased look on his face told me he was not happy to be here.

"Young blood." Hallenbeck smiled. "How's…your lovely lady?"

"Craving chicken nuggets and ice cream."

"For Rita, it was avoc…avocados with chocolate."

"Yo, you win."

They hugged. Why was Hallenbeck so immediately cool toward Ortiz? He was just as much of an ex-criminal as I was, but Hallenbeck never gave him any grief. Was it because Ortiz had sent him a Christmas card?

I clapped to draw their attention.

"Before we get to the plan, Mark, there's one thing you need to understand and agree to." Hallenbeck's brow furrowed. If the smash and grab succeeded, we were going to have to make statements, and we needed to leave Ortiz out of them. I'd wanted to leave lies in the past where they belonged, but I'd tell a thousand lies to protect him from the Sureños.

"Ortiz has a situation," I explained. "To protect his family, he's got a lifetime ban on cooperating with the police. It'd be best if we didn't mention him—ever. I'm not sure how you feel about perjury, but—"

"I get it. No…problem," Hallenbeck said.

"*Chido*," Ortiz said, pleased.

"Good," I said, but it gave me a sour taste in my mouth. The man who'd condemned me for my lies on the fireline had agreed to perjure himself. "It doesn't matter to you that you'd be bending the truth—no, let's be real—straight up lying to the authorities?"

"Yo, what are you doing?" Ortiz cocked his head at me.

"It's fine. I'll…do it."

"And I want you to, because it keeps him safe," I told Hallenbeck. "But I want you to feel *bad* about it. You kept me from being a wildland firefighter because *I* can't be trusted! Because what I do best is lie, cheat, and steal. Well, take a look in the mirror."

Eyes narrowed, Hallenbeck turned over a rock with his cane.

"You have a TBI, for fuck's sake," I spat, bitterness pouring out of me. I stalked over to him. "Anybody else would've shut this down and sent you home. But not me, not after what Graham did to you. My mom was right. You used me." I'd known that all along, but *he* needed to recognize it. He needed to face who he'd become.

Hallenbeck met my gaze, a slight frown on his face. He didn't reply.

"Well?" I snapped.

"I fought…this country's enemies. I fought fires. I used…to *matter*. And that bastard took that from me. This…is an opport… opportunity to matter again. So don't…don't expect an apology."

"I don't want one." It was true. We were finally having the talk, and as much as I should've been furious with him, I couldn't be. "I just want you to remember what you said to Wolfe. Do you remember asking him why he joined CalFire?"

Hallenbeck didn't answer. A piercing *wha-aaaa* call of a coyote sounded from the darkness. An *awhoooo* answered, accompanied by frantic yips and warbles.

"You thought it was because, once, he wanted to protect people. You said that because it's why *you* joined CalFire, isn't it? And why you joined the Marines? That's not why you're doing this now. *This* is coming from the worst place. It's a fire cavity that'll burn you up from the inside out. And it won't stop there. If you fight from *that* place, you'll destroy everything around you and *in you* that's decent."

The hard line of Hallenbeck's mouth twitched, and he looked down, unable to meet my eyes. Ortiz shuffled his feet.

"Sucks I missed this road trip, sounds like it was really fun," he said.

As usual, I couldn't help but smirk. I'd done my best to get through to the old man. I hoped it was enough. *Get going, Mason.* I checked the time. "Two hours until blue hour. No time to waste."

I gave Ortiz a rundown of our gear. Projectile stun guns, gas masks, zip ties, night vision binoculars, and homemade bombs in two varieties. The first was water-bottle dry ice grenades for noise, and the second was what I was calling "blinegar grenades" in glass jars. Neither type had the ingredients mixed yet.

"Blinegar?" Ortiz asked.

"Bleach and vinegar. We have the right amounts set, you just mix them and it makes chlorine gas—"

"This gonna make me an accomplice to murder?"

"First of all, do you think Marshall would report the death of a hired gun protecting his secrets? C'mon. And second, for the amount this'll make, they'd have to sit in it for a half-hour for it to be fatal."

"You did your research."

"The homemade bombs are to cause chaos and 'reduce their combat effectiveness'—his words—" I indicated Hallenbeck, "while we move in with gas masks. We're tasing, hitting, threatening, and zip-tying them out of the game. I'm not trying to kill anybody." I eyed Hallenbeck, who had his cane slung on one shoulder and his rifle slung on the other. "None of us are killing anybody."

"Mace's Mason jars, huh?" Ortiz raised an eyebrow.

"Save the jokes until after the job," I said, failing to stifle a grin. "Those are the tools. This is the plan." I shone a flashlight on my hand-drawn diagram of the tasting room, with a wiggly line for the small creek parallel to it.

"Three gunmen, three entrances. During the day, one was out front, one was at the back door, and the other was in a breakroom on the back side. A breakroom with a window." I pointed to a culvert up the slope. "We follow this to a creek bed that runs parallel to the tasting room. That gets us up there without them seeing us. Me and Hallenbeck kick things off by exploding dry ice bombs near the back door. Bad guys come to check it out, hopefully both of the back area guys, and we gas 'em and zip-tie 'em. Hallenbeck with his rifle out to show 'em we mean business. If the other one is still inside, rinse and repeat. Hallenbeck holds it down while I run to get the car. It's hidden in the woods down the access road. You, you're on the front end. When you hear the first boom, you move in on the guy up front, gas and zip-tie—"

"You're saying that like it's the easiest thing in the world."

"No. But, dude, we've got the element of surprise, chlorine

gas, and *you*. You're a big step up from *mi madre*."

Ortiz shrugged noncommittally.

"You bring down the man in front and move into the building with the hand truck to find the safe. It's a one-story building and I'm betting it's in the room where they keep all the wines. Climate-controlled and all that. I come back with the car, we roll out the safe, load it up together, and bounce."

"You don't know where it is?"

"We've only been able to case the outside."

"You good with all this guesswork?" Ortiz asked Hallenbeck.

"Yes."

Ortiz chewed his nails, taking a moment to process it all.

"Three vs. three, element of surprise," Ortiz summed up.

We knew it wasn't a fair three vs. three, what with Hallenbeck's physical deficits and them shooting to kill. But Hallenbeck and I nodded in agreement with the summary.

"Time to make the donuts," Ortiz said, and held out his fist. I gave it a heartfelt bump.

"I don't deserve you, bro."

"No shit."

We crawled into the culvert, which took us to the creek bed and up the hillside. That extra precaution might've saved our lives, because when we got in sight of the tasting room, the matchup had changed.

"Why is there a dude on the roof with a sniper rifle?" Ortiz asked.

CHAPTER THIRTY-ONE

I looked with the night vision binoculars. The bottom dropped out of my stomach and I forced myself to take measured breaths. There was indeed a man on the front lip of the roof with his own night vision goggles and a sniper rifle. There was also a gunman stationed on the side door, which had been unguarded during the day. In this case, gunwoman—Butch from the church attack. She wore a well-deserved bandage on her nose. That gave us a count of five armed thugs guarding the building.

"Maybe that's what they do at night," I said. *Or maybe it was because of a little brouhaha in downtown Del Rio yesterday.*

The sniper was the biggest threat. I scrambled to think of a way to gas him without him seeing us, but Hallenbeck thought of it first, his mind as fast as his speech was slow.

"We just mod…modify the plan. I'll…go in there." Hallenbeck

pointed to the covered bridge over the creek. "The roof and the fence…give me some concealment. I'll lay down fire on the sniper… drawing his zone of fire this way. Maybe others too. No front and back split. You two both up front. Cover…each other. Gas, breach, zih…zip-tie."

I didn't ask Hallenbeck if he was sure. We were past that. *Someone* had to draw the sniper's attention away from the breachers, and the breachers needed to be fast.

"Five vs. three, and those odds ain't changing unless we kill somebody. You really think we can pull this off?" Ortiz asked.

"We have to try," I said.

"Damn straight. We have two force mult…multipliers. Speed…" Hallenbeck said slowly, "and violence of action."

I hoped he was right.

I nodded and Hallenbeck made his way to the bridge. Ortiz and I moved farther down the creek toward the front of the building. Ortiz held a handgun at the ready, gas mask and non-lethals on his belt, and had the collapsed hand truck strapped to his back. I held one unmixed blinegar grenade at the ready. On my belt I had a gas mask, two stun guns, pepper spray, and a multi-tool. The strap of the bomb bag shifted on my shoulder, the jars and bottles muffled by towels. I pressed it against my ribs to keep it from bouncing, leaving no hands free to stop the gas mask from plinking against the multi-tool.

Ortiz shot me a look.

I mouthed back *I know* and changed my gait to an awkward shuffle to stop the noise. We both squinted at the shape of the gunman stationed at the front entrance, but he hadn't changed position.

Hallenbeck was no longer visible. I didn't know if it was because of the darkness or that he'd made it inside the rustic wooden bridge already. I checked the time.

Crack! Hallenbeck's rifle—he was in the bridge.

He'd moved faster than I expected. I squinted at the building, but couldn't see the sniper rifle muzzle on the lip of the roof. Fumbling in the bag for the night vision binoculars, I swept them up, bashing my nose before I got them to my eyes.

The sniper lifted his rifle away from the front and turned toward the creek. Below him, the gunman out front—Ratface, I recognized—took cover behind a decorative rock formation and looked toward the creek in alarm.

"It worked," I whispered. "Let's move!"

We pulled on our gas masks and charged at the tasting room, noisy gear be damned.

Crack! Hallenbeck fired again, shattering a brick.

Mid-run, I mixed the blinegar grenade and lobbed it—the jar smashed on the rocks, spurting yellow jets in the dark. Ratface jumped back, confused but unaffected, and turned to our pounding footsteps, pistol up—

"Drop it!" Ortiz shouted.

Ratface hesitated.

I pulled the trigger and the stun gun darts clattered in the dark—missed. Keeping my momentum, I ducked under his pistol and slammed him against the rocks. *Violence of action.* Dazed and on the ground, his pistol out of reach, he started coughing. The gas took a minute.

Ortiz zip-tied him before he could regain his senses—

Right as Butch came around the corner, coughing. I raised the second stun gun and fired— *tck-tck-tck-tck*—the weight of her dropping body pulled the wires and almost ripped the stun gun from my hand. I pulled the trigger again—*tck-tck-tck-tck*—and she spasmed, releasing her Uzi. I zip-tied her wrists together.

Two down, three to go.

Tchoo. A silenced rifle shot and the splintering of wood. The sniper had shot back at Hallenbeck.

No no no.

I took two blinegar grenades, shook them hard, and threw them on the roof. They made a satisfying smash. Ortiz grabbed a few dry ice bombs, mixed them, and threw them around the side of the building.

My eyes watered, my lungs burned…my gas mask was askew. Light-headed, I resealed it against my face, mixed two more grenades, and bulled inside…*violence of action*…

I staggered against the wall, dropping one grenade, which rolled away without breaking. Ortiz righted me, just in time— bullets peppered the wall where I'd been. Coughing, blinking rapidly, I fought to clear mucus and tears from my inflamed throat and face and was rewarded with a fogged mask.

Beyond the blurry fog, two gunmen stalked down the hall at us, firing.

We dove behind the tasting bar as wine bottles exploded over our heads.

Ortiz took the other grenade from me and threw it over the bar.

The smash of glass and footsteps approaching.

The gas takes a while...

One gunman reached our side of the bar—

Pop pop pop!

Ortiz's dry ice bombs went off outside, the gunman spun—

Ortiz tackled him in a yellow mist. The other gunman was shooting—I pulled Ortiz down as bullets snapped and used a bar stool to smash the other grenade. Yellow whisps spiraled in the air, and the other gunman coughed and staggered. I knocked the AR from his hands, wrestled him to the floor, and zip-tied his arms behind his back. Ortiz zip-tied the other.

Four down, one to go.

I hadn't heard any more shots from Hallenbeck or from the sniper. Not good.

We hustled from room to room checking for other threats— kitchen, employee bathroom, breakroom, cellar—there was no one. There was also no safe.

Where is it?

Footsteps on the roof thumped toward the edge—we went out the back door and caught the sniper coming down on a ladder, sniffling and coughing. Ortiz and I looked at each other in unspoken agreement and pulled the ladder out from under him. He smacked the ground with a snap and a scream. The bottom half of a shin bone protruded from his skin.

Five down.

As I zip-tied him, I motioned Ortiz at the customer bathrooms—a separate outbuilding.

"Check those."

He shot off and returned in moments.

"All clear. No safe either."

We pulled off our masks. From mine, a glob of snot and saliva plopped in the grass.

"That's fucking disgusting," Ortiz said.

The air was clear around the back end of the building. I breathed deep, trying to clear the bleachy smell of chlorine gas from my nostrils, but it'd taken up residence.

I crouched next to the sniper and hovered my hand over his bloody compound fracture. There was just enough exposed that I could tug it like a lever if need be.

"Tell me where the safe is or I rip this bone out of your leg."

"The kitchen," he coughed, pointing inside.

"No, it's not. We just looked."

I bopped the bone sliver and he spasmed.

"The freezer!" he gasped.

"There was a walk-in in there," Ortiz said.

I nodded.

"My friend, the shooter. Did you get him?"

"I don't know."

The sniper's face was sweaty and snotty. I couldn't tell if he was being honest and didn't have time to suss it out.

"Fine," I said, and stuffed a rag in his mouth. Ortiz zipped duct tape over it. I took a towel out and placed it over the break.

"For the bleeding. Don't try to pop it back in."

I stood up.

"Hallenbeck?" Ortiz asked.

"Mission first. You get the safe, I'll get the car. He might already be on the way."

Or he might be dead. I hoped to God that wasn't the case.

I checked the time. It'd been seven minutes since Hallenbeck fired the first shot. We'd made a lot of noise. Any of these guys might've called or texted for backup, and there was also the possibility that someone in the surrounding hills had called the police. We needed to move *fast*.

I ran down the access road and into the woods. The truck was untouched. The suspension rattled something fierce as I jostled the vehicle back to the road, gunning it up to the tasting room. Got it in place and hopped out, fighting cramps to jog around to the side facing the creek.

"Hallenbeck?" I hissed.

A coyote yipped in the distance. A metallic hammering sounded from inside the building. Something rustled. I prickled from the feeling of being watched but didn't see anyone.

I rushed toward the creek. Hallenbeck hadn't made his way outside the bridge, it seemed. I went inside and found him shirtless, his butt on the floor, his back against the railing, and the rifle at his feet. He wasn't moving.

"Mark?"

I knelt down next to him and his eyes snapped open. He lurched for the rifle, then stopped.

"Scared...the shit out of me," he said.

"You scared the shit out of *me*!"

"Taking a rest. Had...had to plug a hole." He'd turned his shirt into a makeshift bandage wrapped around his upper chest. Even in the dark, the blood spot was visible.

"Jesus," I said.

Hallenbeck tapped a wooden post with a wicked, splintered hole.

"It was a bounce. If it…was direct? Be a diff…different story." His eyes went wide at something behind me. "Behind—!"

I turned to a blur of motion and threw up my arms—

Thock! The world split into pieces and I slumped against the planks. Butch…rock…forehead… My left arm had collided with her swinging right and absorbed the brunt of the force, but the rock in her hand had still made contact. If I hadn't turned… I lurched up, senses coalescing and splintering and coalescing again.

Crack!

Butch twisted, grunting, but kept coming, and before Hallenbeck could fire again, she was on him. I shoved her and she toppled over. The world flew up at me and I was back on the planks, head spinning.

Hallenbeck straddled her and held the rifle like a bar, pushing the barrel against her throat. She rasped and battered his arms, but he was locked in. Neck corded, nostrils flaring, spittle frothing from heated breaths.

"Mark."

The moment stretched. And stretched. And stretched.

Hallenbeck pulled back. He gulped in a massive breath, met my gaze, and sat down hard.

"Help me…with her."

"Happy to."

How she'd gotten free I didn't know, but I tied her up for the second time, adding multiple ties and anchoring her to the planks.

I put a rag and duct tape over the bullet hole Hallenbeck had scored on her arm and kicked away the river rock she'd hit me with.

"Hurts, doesn't it?" she laughed bitterly.

I decided to put a rag and duct tape over her mouth too.

Doing my best to ignore the flaring pain she'd left in my forehead, I clasped Hallenbeck's shoulder. He put a hand on mine and squeezed it, finger muscles trembling as he fought to keep hold. My eyes got misty. *The real Hallenbeck just stood up.*

"Let's help Ortiz," I husked, throat froggy.

We staggered to the kitchen. Ortiz turned, stopping short of bashing my face in with a fire extinguisher.

"Yo, what the fuck! Announce yourself."

"Sorry."

The walk-in freezer door was one of the big silver kind with a horizontal handle. It also had a lock and fresh dents from where Ortiz had been hitting it with the base of the fire extinguisher.

He struck it again, denting and shifting the handle, but it remained on the door.

"I got this," I grinned, and like a rabbit from a hat, I brought a blowtorch from the bag. Putting the nozzle against the bolts, I pressed the red button.

Click. No flame. I pressed the button again. Nothing. I tightened the propane connection and pressed the button repeatedly. Nothing.

"Ain't happening. Next, please!" Ortiz said.

"I've got an idea."

Using a towel to protect my hands, I took a piece of pure dry ice from my bag and wrapped it around the handle with the towel.

White vapor filled the pantry as the solid turned to gas.

Ortiz tottered, and I pulled him back.

"That's pure...carbon dioxide," Hallenbeck said.

"Fuck." We stood back, getting light-headed. We probably shouldn't be sitting with it, but we had to.

The metal tinked from the change in temperature.

"Now?"

"One more second," I said. "Okay."

THUNK! Ortiz walloped the handle with the fire extinguisher and it broke off completely, the freezer door yawning open. Kicking fragments of dry ice every which way, we stepped inside. The freezer wasn't on, and there were only two things in it.

A box of crackers and the safe.

"Yes!" I shouted.

"We...got it," Hallenbeck grinned.

"Then let's fucking go," Ortiz said.

We did.

CHAPTER THIRTY-TWO

An orange glow stretched from below the horizon, merging with a bruised purple sky. I drove us and our trophy back to the De La Uva campground. The safe sat in the truck bed, barely sliding, but I wasn't breathing easy yet. My eyes were on it vibrating in the rearview more than the road ahead. Hallenbeck sat next to me, and Ortiz followed in my Ducati, which he'd used to get here. Hallenbeck's wound had stopped bleeding.

I stopped at an outcrop of sandstone boulders jutting two stories high. The boulders had craggy recesses, broken stacks, and deep shadows.

"This is it."

Ortiz and I two-man carried the safe to a deep recess on the far side and deposited it in the darkness. We weighted a tarp over it to protect from animals and weather. Hallenbeck kept watch.

We scrutinized our path, breaking up dirt where we'd left tracks, spreading leaves, and even checked the bushes for clothes fuzz. As we went, I noticed blisters and burns bulging from the stitched cut on my forearm. Had to be the gas. *Hoisted by my own fuckin' petard.* A grassfire burned across my skin.

Breathe, Mason. Almost there.

Clear. The safe and our path to it were invisible from the road. Still, I didn't breathe easy. Not until we returned to our own campsite and inspected the area. The fishing line we'd put up as a perimeter remained undisturbed, and our tents and everything in them were exactly as we'd left them. Finally, the high-tension wires in my body released. The air filling my lungs was bracing and clean.

I hugged Ortiz.

"Thank you."

"*No hay bronca,*" he said, as if all he'd done was buy me a beer. Then he grinned and bounced over to the firepit, letting out a gleeful whoop. "Cold now that we're not running around. I'ma get a fire going."

Eyes twinkling, Hallenbeck held out his hand. There was no tremor there as I shook it.

"Well done," he said.

"You too."

I wished the deserter was here to see this. She thought it was insane? A lost cause? Not for two ex-cons and a TBI victim. Ortiz had delivered. Hallenbeck had been clutch. *We did it.* I was not just the man who had endangered Ash River and left Hallenbeck broken. The world would know that Mason Jones was not a murderer. I would be the man who exposed the real murderer, a man responsible for the destruction of 15,217 homes and the deaths of 29 people.

My legs were rubber and I sat down hard. Hands trembling, skin tingling.

"Holy shit. Holy shit."

I did it.

Ortiz fed logs to a flickering fire. I savored the warmth and the heartening smell of woodsmoke for a spell. Then I took my original phone out of its Faraday pocket and powered it on. The number I needed was 1-800-CALL-FBI. Go figure. My muscles tensed back up. This wasn't going to be easy.

"It's time to call the FBI," I said.

"Time for me to go then," Ortiz said. He exaggerated a frown at the fire he'd started and wouldn't get to enjoy.

"I can wait…" I shouldn't, but I didn't want to rush him after all he'd done tonight.

"Naw. Don't wait. Get it done."

Hallenbeck nodded in agreement. "Joshua, don't…keep a good woman waiting. We'll…protect you."

Ortiz grinned and walked to the motorcycle. He shot me a look. "Next time you see her, you're gonna tell her how super well-behaved and safe I was tonight."

I grinned back and watched him drive down the road.

I went back to Hallenbeck at the campfire, warmed my hands, and got out my phone again.

"You ready?"

He nodded.

A loud snapping sounded from down the road. I knew that

sound: tires popping. Then, overlapping shouts. A male and female voice—and Ortiz's.

Hallenbeck reached for his rifle, wincing, but I dropped the phone and grabbed it instead.

I sprinted down the winding forest road, slinging gravel in my wake. The Ducati had slid into a wall of trees, both tires blown out by a spike strip. Agent Luo had Ortiz cuffed and bent over the hood of their sedan, while Agent Prescott stood next to the car, her weapon pointed at me.

"Drop the rifle!" she shouted.

"Let him go," I said, pointing the weapon at Prescott. If I shot first, before she shot me, and Ortiz tackled Luo, maybe we could make it out of this. I didn't know if I could actually do it—but for Ortiz? Both agents wore ballistic vests. If I did it, I'd have to go for her head.

Luo pushed Ortiz down and drew on me. I turned the rifle his direction. He was more dangerous.

"Easy, Kevin," Prescott told him.

Kevin. Boone's once up on a time, based in NorCal Kevin? The Kevin she was supposed to meet up with after taking us in?

Sweat beaded on my forehead as my mind raced. It *was* that Kevin. The man holding a torch for DAPO Agent Jasmine Boone was California DOJ Agent Kevin Luo. *That's why they were out for blood.*

It didn't seem like *they* were though. Just him. At the parade, Prescott had yelled at Luo to holster his weapon. That was probably more for the bystanders' sakes than mine, and yet she seemed to be trying to rein him in now too. What was Prescott's part in this?

Could she get me and Ortiz out of this alive?

Luo's face was stormy but his hands were steady. He wasn't pulling the trigger. They hadn't shot Ortiz, they'd cuffed him. What was this? An arrest? An interrogation? An execution?

Hallenbeck's rifle was an electrified conduit in my hands. If I broke the connection, would it bring life or death?

"Drop it," Prescott repeated.

I dropped the rifle and kicked it away. If they were going to shoot us, they already would've. She took out her own set of cuffs and slapped them on me, cinching them so tight my hands purpled.

"Walk," Prescott said. Taking charge, she perp-walked us back to the campsite. Ortiz shot me a harried look. Hallenbeck had the phone in his hands, the keypad glowing white with a full string of black numbers on it.

"Put the phone down, please," she said.

"It's the FBI. Given your history…with my friend, I think it's…for the best."

Hallenbeck hit the green dial button.

Prescott marched over, pinned him down, and ripped the phone from his hand. He gasped and held a hand to his chest.

A tinny female voice issued from the speaker, "FBI tip line, if this is an emergency, please dial 9-1-1. How may I—"

She threw the phone to the ground and fired a bullet into it. It rocked and went dark, a web of shattered glass ringing a smoking hole in its center.

"Tina…" Luo said.

"Shut up and watch my six, Kevin," she said.

Luo gaped as Prescott handcuffed Hallenbeck around a tree,

and then did the same to Ortiz, and then me. The carbon steel bit into my wrists, forcing me to bear-hug a gnarled trunk. We were helpless. My body went cold. *What the hell is going on?*

Prescott went to the truck first, then strolled around the campsite, looking through the tents and the gear. She peered at the surrounding forest, the rising sun casting long shadows off the trees.

"Where's the safe?" she asked.

What? How they even knew about the safe, I didn't know, but I couldn't risk telling them. No rights had been read; they weren't arresting us.

"It's gone," I said.

"Where?"

"Somewhere safe." There's nothing quite like an Abbott and Costello routine at gunpoint.

"*Where?*" she repeated.

Luo cocked his head at her. "What safe? What are you talking about?"

He didn't know about the safe…only she did. Which could mean only one thing. My heart hammered dully in my chest and my legs shook.

Ortiz set his feet against his tree and pulled. The cuffs cut into the bark, but the tree barely wobbled. I pulled against my own, but it was useless. Hallenbeck sank down the tree he was cuffed to, grunting.

Prescott smiled grimly and came over to him, eyeing the bandage on his upper chest. It was red with fresh blood. She pressed the barrel of her pistol to the center of it, and he hissed in pain.

"The location of the safe, please."

Hallenbeck grimaced but said nothing.

She jammed it down harder. Hallenbeck cried out and wobbled on his knees.

"Come on, now."

"Fuck...off," he grunted.

Prescott *tsked* him and turned to Ortiz, then to me.

"Anyone? Let's not make this difficult. Tell me where the safe is and this can be over."

"What he said, bitch," Ortiz said.

Prescott pistol-whipped him, leaving a smear of Hallenbeck's blood on his forehead.

Luo watched in shock.

"Your boss isn't getting away with murder again," I said.

"What is he talking about?" Luo asked.

She ignored him and stepped back to a tactical distance, pointing her gun at me with one hand. With the other, she brought a radio to her lips.

"Dispatch, this is CBI Agent 2106. Request assistance at 3000 De La Uva Way, Del Rio. Again, request for assistance at a campground just southeast of Redhorn Winery. I have eyes on an armed POI holding hostages, suspected kidnapping to avoid arrest. POI is threatening hostages. Positive ID: POI is Mason Jones."

"What the hell?" Luo said.

"You were going to officer-involved-murder him. I don't want to hear it."

"You're out of your depth, Kevin," I said. Poor bastard had just wanted to avenge his ex, and here his partner was working for a corrupt billionaire.

"Tina, you need to tell me what the hell is going on."

"California is broken, and the man I work for is one of the few people trying to fix it. That's what's going on," Prescott snapped.

Luo stood in a daze, staring. His weapon was pointed at the ground, forgotten.

She clipped the radio back to her belt and took out a phone. Her contact answered on the first dial.

"Boss, we need that leverage," she said.

A deep, resonant voice answered.

"We're here. Does he have it?" the voice asked.

"Yes. He's hiding it."

"Turn it around."

She turned the phone around. It was a video call, and on-screen was the man behind it all. I'd only ever seen pictures and video of him.

"Let's cut to the chase, Mason," Erik Marshall said, salt and pepper hair at his temples catching staggered lines of light. Window blinds.

Marshall turned his own phone, and I saw a motel room blur by before the camera settled and focused on a view of Emily and Vee cowering, their faces puffy from crying, beneath Jasmine Boone's killer, the silver-haired Curione. An icy jolt ripped me from head to tail: Vee's shirt was spackled with brown-red blood, and Curione's pants were slick with it. *Whose blood? What have they done to them?*

"No no no…" Ortiz murmured in horror.

"The blood is the dog's, but that can change," Marshall said.

"Please, don't, we can—" I began.

"Hurt her," Marshall ordered, cutting me off.

Curione punched Vee in her baby bump.

She doubled over and wailed in pain. Emily burst into fresh tears.

"Stop! We can deal!" I screamed.

"Not yet," Marshall said.

Vee curled up on the floor as Curione kicked her again and again. Emily wailed incoherently.

"Please!" I screamed.

"Please!" Ortiz howled, pulling against his restraints in impotent rage, tears cutting ravines through the dust on his face.

"Baby!" Vee cried, hearing her man's voice.

"Stop!" I screamed.

Hallenbeck surged to his feet and Prescott shoved him back down, his head knocking against his tree.

"Please," I pleaded.

On-screen, Marshall held up a finger and Curione stopped.

Emily crawled to her mother, and they held each other, sobbing.

I didn't even wait for him to ask.

"It's in a bunch of boulders down the road," I gasped. "Sandstone. Far side."

"Kevin, go," Prescott said.

Luo's face was pale, but his jaw was set.

"No," he said.

"Find the safe and you can finally smoke this dirtbag."

"No."

He raised his gun…toward her.

"Enough," he said.

Hope fluttered in my chest. *Come on, Jasmine's boyfriend...*

Blam! Thwap! It was a blur—she was *fast*—and Luo was on the ground, blood spurting from his neck. Prescott shook her head. "Sorry, Kevin."

The air went out of my lungs. Bark chewed up my forehead as I slumped against the tree.

"Verifying," Prescott said into the phone, and marched down the road.

Ortiz wilted against his tree, sniffling. Then he snarled and used his cuffs to saw at the tree. Tiny bits of bark and yellow slivers fell to the ground, but the progress was miniscule. It'd take hours to make a real dent. We had only minutes left to live. Ortiz stopped sawing, sobbed, then started again. Then he stopped for good. His head against the bark, he cried softly.

Bile rising in my throat, heart thundering in my ears, I strained against the cuffs. I only succeeded in bruising my wrists. I shook tears from my stinging eyes. There was no way the baby survived—Curione had taken Ortiz's child away with that beating. Because of me.

For the first time in 15 years, I'd set out to do good. I'd tried to do everything the right way. "*Destroy his world,*" Hallenbeck had said. I'd rejected that battle cry and found a fugitive from justice. I'd called a cop, Jasmine Boone, to bring his evidence to light, and she'd been gunned down for it. At every step, I'd tried to do right, to think about the domino effect, to spare innocents. Refusing to kill. And where had it got me?

Emily and Vee were bloodied hostages. Her pregnancy

violently ended, and Penny was dead. Ortiz was a crazed mess. Dizzy, I leaned against the tree with acid saliva filling my mouth. I couldn't stop spitting.

Not enough skin.

I thought I could right my wrongs. But my mother, the addict, had been right. Sometimes you can't make amends. What happened to Hallenbeck, what happened to Ash River…happened. Nothing I could do would ever *undo* it. The epiphany was like a cold knife to the heart. And, of course, like any life-changing epiphany, it seemed obvious in hindsight. My stomach heaved, but there was nothing in it. All I could do was spit and gag at the caustic bile in my throat.

I looked at Hallenbeck. His bandage had sopped off and the wound wept burgundy tears. His face was a mask of regret. We'd been so close. All that was left of our efforts was the bullet-shattered phone at his feet.

A phone with a lithium-ion battery that was only a few feet from the crackling campfire.

"The phone!" I said, nodding at it with my head.

Hallenbeck goggled at me, not understanding.

Footsteps. Tina Turncoat was returning.

"Kick the phone in the fire!" I hissed.

Hallenbeck's eyes lit up. Grimacing in concentration, contorting his body away from the tree, he used a quivering foot to scoop the phone and flip it through the air. It landed in the flames with a shower of sparks.

Prescott stalked back into the campground, satisfaction on her face. Focused on her own phone, she didn't notice the other, its plastic and glass warping in the fire.

"I'll load it up right away," she said.

She stood with her back to the fire, watching us. Something popped, but nothing burst from the flames. Maybe nothing would.

"Let them go," I said. "You got what you want. Please."

"Goodbye, Mason," Marshall said, ending the call.

Prescott brought out the radio again and blinked rapidly, her face shifting. Getting into the role.

"Agent down! Agent down, suspect is firing on the hostages! I'm going in."

She's thorough, I thought dully.

She pointed her gun at me.

I locked eyes with Ortiz.

"I'm sorry I dragged you into this."

Then I faced her, ready.

Please, get me in the head. Make it quick.

Pop-fwoom! A pillar of fire exploded behind her. Prescott staggered and slumped into a crouch, her back riddled with cinders, smoke weaving in tendrils around her. She coughed and groaned, wobbling.

Then she stood back up. Smoke rippled from a piece of shrapnel in her hair bun, her bare arms were covered with burns, and she had a grim smile on her face.

"'A' for effort," she said, and raised her gun again.

Crack!

Prescott toppled on her feet and smacked the ground, her eyes sightless, blood seeping from her skull.

My mother stood across the campground behind her, Hallenbeck's rifle in her hand.

CHAPTER THIRTY-THREE

Throat constricting, vision blurring, I turned away as Kit rushed over.

"You should've let her do it," I said.

"Don't say that!"

A clinking sound—she took the keys off Prescott's corpse and unlocked my cuffs. My hands tingled painfully.

"Would've been better," I said.

Smack. Her slap made the tears spatter all over me.

"No," she said, and ran on to Hallenbeck and Ortiz.

I stayed where I was. All I could see was Emily and Vee holding each other, sobbing.

A gurgle.

I jerked to my feet and peered at Prescott. Very dead. I ran over to Luo. He'd clamped his hand to his neck, and while God knows how many pints of his blood soaked the ground beneath him, he was still breathing. His eyes widened at me.

"Hold on." I looked around.

Ortiz was running down the road, but Kit and Hallenbeck remained. He massaged his wrists, and Kit was helping him reapply the bandage to his wound.

Triage. Luo's wound was more serious.

"Mom, bring me the first aid kit. Give Hallenbeck your phone. Hallenbeck, call for an ambulance for both of you."

Kit got the first aid kit from the truck and brought it to me.

We were out of homeostatic dressings. I was gonna have to do this the old-fashioned way.

"This is gonna hurt," I told Luo, ripping gauze out of their packets. I took his hand off his neck and blood gurgled from a red trench perpendicular to the line of his throat. Entrance wound by the throat, exit on the side of his neck. The bullet had gone more across than through, but given the blood loss it had probably hit his carotid. I packed gauze on it, pressing firmly, feeling with my fingers—there, a loss of skin resistance, where the warm blood emanated from—pressing as much of the gauze as I could into the void, hands growing sticky, I kept packing more as the layers soaked through. Luo grunted and squeezed his eyes shut, taking the pain stoically.

"…carotid arter… artery trauma," Hallenbeck was saying into the phone. He was present and calm. Between his joints and the gunshot wound, I couldn't imagine the pain the guy was in. "Bleeding…profusely, putting pressure on it. Packing gauze. That's…patient one. Second patient, up…upper chest trauma.

Bleed…bleeding but not heavy."

I kept packing and pressing until the bleeding slowed. I held two bloody fingers over his face. He blinked at me.

"How many?"

"Two," he breathed, barely audible. He gazed at me in astonishment. "Thank you."

"Uh-huh. Don't move."

I motioned Kit at the gauze I was holding. "Take over for me. Firm pressure."

I tended to Hallenbeck. It wasn't a gusher, and as soon as I rebandaged it I scrambled to my next task: scouring the campground for the phone Prescott had been using. If I kept moving, I wouldn't see Emily and Vee crumpled and sobbing.

I found it. It was locked, but her eyes were still open and her face was still intact. It beeped, unlocking, and I set it to stay that way. I took her gun, too, and paused to look at Hallenbeck, Kit, and Luo. The shrill howl of a siren echoed in the distance. Couldn't be the ambulance already…it had to be the police Prescott had called.

"Keep the pressure on his wound until the ambulance gets here. I have to go." Would Kit and Hallenbeck be safe? How many others were on Marshall's payroll? Lightheaded with worry, I indicated Kit's phone. "Call the FBI. Tell them everything. Make sure any cops that show up *know* you called the FBI." That was all I could do for them.

Hallenbeck nodded in understanding, but Kit stared at me with dinner plate eyes, her mouth an open frown.

"What are you doing?" Kit asked.

I tried to stand, but my knees buckled and I collapsed back to a crouch by Prescott's body. The world went blurry again. *She came back.* I let myself feel the fullness in my chest for a moment, just a moment, and pistoning to my feet, I said:

"Helping my friend."

Struck by an idea, I crouched by Luo again, patting down his pockets until I found his keys. "You have emergency flashers, right? A siren? It'll be faster."

He clamped a hand on mine, stopping me. Kit fought to keep the gauze in place. He stared at me for three agonizing seconds. "Glovebox," he murmured, releasing my hand and nodding at me to go.

"Thank you," I said, hoping my eyes said everything I couldn't. *For not killing me, for trying, and for these.* I took the keys and drove the truck down the road.

Ortiz was tugging the spike strip off the road. On the other side of it sat what I guessed was the rental car Kit had returned in. I helped him heave the strip into the underbrush and showed him the keys to the sedan. Multiple sirens pierced the air now, and one was getting closer.

Ortiz froze in place, breathing shakily. "Mace, what if…"

"Don't." I gripped his arm. "They're more useful to him alive."

I held out Prescott's phone to him. It was ready to dial the most recent contact.

He pressed dial. Marshall answered, voice-only this time.

"What's your ETA?" he asked.

"This is Joshua Ortiz. I'm bringing the safe. Don't hurt my family anymore."

A barely controlled breath sounded from the line as Marshall weighed the change in fortune.

"You better be quick then," he said, and hung up.

Once we loaded the safe in the truck, Ortiz got in its driver's seat. I took the agents' sedan. The approaching siren jabbing our ears now, we pulled the vehicles behind the rock formation as a Del Rio Police SUV barreled down the road strobing red and blue. When it was past, we shot out of the campground and onto the highway before more could arrive.

Even with the siren and emergency lights, it took us 38 excruciating minutes to get to the Castaic motel where Ortiz had sequestered his family. How had Marshall and Curione found them?

I turned off the alert systems two minutes before we arrived and let Ortiz pass me. I parked down the road and watched him pull into the boxy motel complex's single inlet/outlet. I grabbed a shotgun off the back seat, and I also had Prescott's gun tucked in the seat of my pants. A chill shivered up my spine, raising goosebumps on my arms. I'd been here before. A cold monster with a bloody trade offer. A possession on one scale, the life of a loved one on the other. *Lives*, this time.

Was I cursed? Would anyone I cared about ever be safe?

The motel complex was a giant two-story rectangle with a parking lot courtyard, and Ortiz's family had been on the end opposite the entrance. Second floor, Room 221. I entered the complex through a corner stairway, making my way upstairs, and watched Ortiz park. It was 8 in the morning, and there were no bystanders around. Good.

Curione and a man with a dark and scruffy beard came out of Room 221 and onto the second-floor walkway. They looked down at Ortiz. Even with no one around, they were cautious. Loose jackets concealed their weapons, and they kept their hands at their sides.

"Where's Jones?" Curione asked.

"Your pet cop shot him."

Curione narrowed his eyes, skeptical. I ducked behind a soda machine as his gaze went around the complex. Apparently satisfied, he motioned at the safe, which was covered in a tarp in the truck bed.

"Take off the tarp. Let's see it."

"Proof of life first," Ortiz said, his voice strangled.

They were all the way across the complex from me. I began creeping that direction.

Impatient, Curione flicked his hand at his counterpart, and the bearded man went inside and dragged Vee to the window. She was pale and listless. At best, in shock. At worst, bleeding internally.

"My daughter too, bitch!" Ortiz shouted.

The man held up Emily behind the window.

"Daddy!" her voice came muffled through the window.

"I'm coming, *mija*," he said.

He shoved the girl down.

Ortiz climbed into the truck bed and tore off the tarp.

"Boss," Curione said.

Marshall himself stepped out to look at it. He spoke with Curione, who was peering closely at the safe. They were making sure it was the same one his crew had taken from us at the church.

Ortiz glared venomously at them.

"Daddy! Da—!" Emily cried again, a slap cutting her off. "Quiet!" someone hissed. She whimpered. I was almost there, and I could hear it all now, walls or not. *I'm coming, sweetie.*

Curione pointed to the swooping scratch on the side of the safe and gave Marshall a confirming nod. This was Wolfe's safe. Marshall and Curione walked back into the room, stepping aside as the bearded man came out holding an assault rifle with a black tube on the bottom of it.

A grenade launcher.

Ortiz's eyes widened and he dove away—

Shunk! Boom!

The truck bed disappeared in an orange blast, and the gunner didn't stop there. *Pop! Crack! Ping!* Bullets ripped into the truck.

They weren't here to trade.

I sprinted to the gunner and flipped him over the balcony, pivoting toward the door to Room 221 as it shut in my face. I hit the deck—splinters showered my back as bullets tore through the door. Staying flat, I looked below.

The gunner was groaning next to the truck—broken legs, it looked like. Ortiz appeared as a tank-topped blur, moving out from behind the truck cab and firing three rounds in the gunner's head. He spat on the pulpy remnants of the man's head and rushed to the stairway.

The truck bed itself was a white-hot inferno. The face of the safe glowed orange, with a fissure that spewed sparking, racing flames. Molten streams ran out from it, pooling, smoking, and eating through the metal below. The only thing I knew capable of that was thermite. Marshall had spared no expense.

The evidence against him—Wolfe's insurance policy, my ticket to a clean slate—billowed into the sky as acrid smoke.

None of that mattered.

Ortiz came out of the stairway onto the walkway. I motioned at the room next-door, 219, and pointed to myself. He nodded and I tossed him the shotgun. He blasted the 221 doorknob off and jumped aside as a hail of return fire whizzed out. I took out Prescott's service weapon and kicked in the other door.

The bad guys were already moving through 219. I'd meant to use the room to come at them via the adjoining side-door, but two of them were using it to take Vee and Emily away—useful leverage until Marshall was clear.

I bulled into the first one, who was dragging Vee by her hair, and the one behind him carrying Emily stepped back—right as Ortiz burst through the side door and shot him in the head.

Emily screamed.

I held the pistol over the man who'd been dragging Vee. He was on the floor, his hands raised.

"Please, don't—"

Ortiz shot him too.

No other enemies here. I peered in 221, where they'd come from, and it was also clear. I didn't see Penny's body.

Where were Marshall and Curione?

I ran to the bathroom, which had a frosted window above the toilet. It was open, and there were scuff marks on the toilet.

Son of a bitch.

I turned back around to see Ortiz on his knees, tears streaming down his face, his arms wrapped around his family.

"Daddy," Emily sobbed into his shoulder.

"I'm here, *mija.*"

Vee was still in shock, and Ortiz gave her a once over. He lifted her shirt up to see deep purple bruising on her belly and ribs. He twitched and clenched his fists…and then unclenched them, drawing on some inner strength to put on a kind, comforting face for them. He held Emily close and stroked Vee's shoulders. Her thousand-yard stare began to melt, and her eyes began to move around behind their wall of tears.

"Babe," she said, and threw herself into him. He squeezed her tight.

"Where's Penny?" Ortiz asked softly.

"I was outside, taking her to potty, when—when they…" She choked up.

Ortiz nodded and stroked her head, his hand trembling. With rage, it seemed.

"I'm going after Marshall," I said.

"Let's go," he replied, standing and taking up the shotgun again, his knuckles white on the grip.

"Just me. Get your family to the hospital."

His eyes cleared, what truly mattered breaking through the red he was seeing. I knew the feeling. He nodded.

"And gimme those." I took the shotgun and his pistol, wiping the handles and triggers with my shirt. Then I wrapped my hand around them and firmly pressed my fingers on their warm metal bodies.

Ortiz eyed me but didn't remark on that. Instead, he said, "Good luck."

Taking his ladies' hands, he led them out of the room.

Marshall was probably long gone by now, but I raced out and leapt down the stairs. What would I do if I caught them?

Behind the motel was a vacant lot choked with tall grass and weeds, with a path that had been stamped down by Marshall's retreat. All the way across it, Marshall and Curione ran toward a black SUV parked at the curb.

While running, I fired a wild shot at the vehicle. The two stopped and ducked, looking back—and at the same time, the world flipped and I landed on my face. One gunman waited in the tall grass, covering Marshall's retreat. He pointed his rifle at me.

"Wait!" I shouted, and threw down my weapons. "I want to deal!"

Marshall scoffed, but he signaled to the rifleman, and he led me at barrel-point to Marshall and Curione. Two more armed thugs came out of the SUV and surrounded us. With Curione, that made four guns to none, since I'd given mine up.

Curione's face was a focused grimace. His knuckles, arms, and clothes were still bloody. I could hear Vee and Emily wailing when I looked at him. I gagged as he frisked me but kept still.

"He's clean."

Marshall had a single spot of blood on his khakis, but otherwise looked the part of a distinguished professional, with his square jaw and fitted polo. His eyes were light brown and his gaze was piercing.

I wanted to rip them apart. But this wasn't about me. It wasn't about making up for my past, or even my future. I didn't know what I'd do, but I knew I had to make sure the people I loved stopped suffering.

"I'm more useful to you alive than dead," I said.

"Be serious, Mason. Whatever you thought you had on me is up in smoke. You have no cards left to play."

His composure, his commanding confidence. That deep voice. It made me sick.

"I can keep you clean. That's what this is all about, isn't it? Burning every thread connecting you to the Patchwork."

A line creased his brow—just barely.

"But there's a mess of threads now," I continued. "California DOJ agents on the payroll. *Dead cops.*" I gestured behind me. "Military-grade explosives and more bodies."

"What's your offer?"

"I'll take the blame. For all of it. I'll go along with whatever your fixer here says to make it work and swear to it in front of a judge. I got only one condition: the people I care about are untouchable. Out of bounds. Safe, forever."

"All of it," Marshall said, nodding minutely as if satisfied.

This was the most important conversation of my life. I studied every turn of his mouth, his tone, his breathing. Every twitch of his eyelids, because his gaze didn't move off me. The coloring of his face. If you're good, and I'm pretty good, you can find someone's tell.

His was the same as mine. Strong eye contact. He was *willing* his mark to believe him.

"Can you stomach it? *That* lie?" he asked. "One thing I learned from that Grayson business: you're not a killer."

People keep telling me that, I thought.

"I can stomach it for them. That means you guarantee the safety of Ortiz and his family. Hallenbeck and his. My mother." In a flash of inspiration, I added another name to the list.

"Even Sean Wolfe," I said. Marshall didn't know I knew he was dead.

He squinted at me, a soft *hmm* sounding in his throat. He held out his hand.

"Deal," he said.

How can you guarantee the safety of a man you had killed? There was no deal. And there was only one way I could be sure that those I loved would be safe.

I clasped his hand and yanked down, digging my hands into his hair to hold him as I kneed his throat savagely—once, twice, three, four times before they dragged me away, fists smacking my face, feet pummeling my stomach…but it was too late. As I laid on the ground reeling from a boot in the ribs, Marshall reached for his caved-in throat, groaned, and died.

"Fuck," Curione murmured.

The others' attacks slowed, then stopped as they reeled in shock. I sat up from the ground and they encircled me. Their guns were on me, but their eyes were wide, and their attention was torn between me and their dead boss.

The high-pitched wail of a siren echoed in the distance.

"Do we smoke him?" one of them asked Curione. They all looked to Curione now.

I focused my gaze on him too.

"It's done. He can't pay you. He can't threaten you. He has no power over you."

The siren was getting louder.

"You could kill me, but what's the point?" I asked. "Who's gonna pay you for it? Who's gonna make sure it's wrapped up nice and clean?"

They hesitated.

"I'm not going anywhere, but you can," I said, getting cross-legged to be more comfortable. Calm as could be, I added, "They're getting close."

"Fuck this," Curione said, and with a final glare at me, he ran to the SUV. The others followed, and it barreled off down the street and disappeared around a corner.

Beneath the piercing sound of the approaching siren, there was another high-pitched sound. It was quieter, and halting, but somehow audible. It was close by.

I tramped through the weeds and found a gray lump in a congealed puddle of blood. Dazedly, I got down on my knees and realized it was Penny. I put one hand in front of her muzzle and the other on her abdomen. Moist air tickled one hand, and the abdomen rose and fell—minutely but rapidly. Her tail flopped once and she whined again. Did she recognize me?

She had a gunshot wound in her head. How the hell was she alive? I bent closer. The bullet had come in right above the eye and chinked out through the jaw. Somehow, it hadn't gone through the brain. She was in shock, but alive! My chest warmed and I had to wipe my eyes to get a clear look.

The entrance wound above her eye had clotted on its own, and the exit in her jaw was encrusted with grime—she'd rubbed it in dirt, probably in pain, and it had helped stop the bleeding.

I got out my phone and called the fancy animal shelter where Ortiz worked. It was in West LA, an hour away, but I told them it was Penny. He'd adopted her from that shelter and she got all her checkups there. A veterinarian named Sara promised to send a Castaic vet she trusted right over. I thanked her and ended the call.

Bone tired, I stroked Penny and waited, the sirens piercing now, the lights visible down the street.

"I'll stay with you as long as I can, girl."

CHAPTER THIRTY-FOUR

The conference room AC was busted. It was stuffy. Gail, my public defender, had said her piece and left me alone with my mother. A coffee machine without a carafe dripped onto its hot plate. *Sst. Sst. Sst.* The carpet was the exact same color as the rotted one in Wolfe's church. Here, instead of dripping holes, it had bald spots where chairs had worn it to the pad.

"How are you doing with everything?" I asked.

"I don't like your options, but there's nothing we can do about it."

"That's not what I was asking."

Kit didn't answer, instead deciding the folders on the table needed shuffling.

Luo had put in a statement saying Kit's shot was justified. She would not be charged for Prescott's death. That wasn't why I tensed with concern.

"I have nightmares," I told her. The crunch of his windpipe. The whites of his eyes, the whimpering groan. His last breath. The first time I had the nightmare, after throwing up and tossing my sweat-soaked sheets on the cell floor, I was relieved. It meant I wasn't a psychopath.

Then it kept coming back.

"I'm having some too," she said, and shuddered.

"You saved my life. You saved all of us." I reached out my hand. She took it. "That doesn't make it easy."

She nodded.

"I'm sorry."

"I'm not." She squeezed my hand. "I don't regret it."

I have the nightmare almost every night now, but I don't regret what I did, either. Ortiz and his girls are safe. Mom is safe. Hallenbeck and his family are safe. I don't regret what I did, but I wonder when the nightmares will go away. Or if they ever will.

Something else though. The voice that had haunted me, that had been loudest in the night? It was gone. I knew who I was now.

"Are you going to be able to, um…?"

"Stay clean?" Kit smiled faintly. "Yes. It's different this time." Sniffling, she dabbed her eyes. She cleared her throat. "How about we get back to the matter at hand?"

"My plea? This whole thing? Guess we could go over it," I said. I had a decision to make. The visions I'd written into my *After This* notebook grew dim and a heaviness I'd been fighting to contain uncoiled in my chest. "What do *you* think?"

"Do my ears deceive me? You want to know what *I* think?"

Her smile was teasing, but there was a sadness behind it.

"Is it so crazy to think you might have some wisdom to offer?" I teased back.

"Whatever you decide, whatever happens, I'll support you."

"C'mon. I know you have an opinion."

"Just be honest," she said.

I hugged her tight. These days, that was occasionally a thing. And maybe it was because of Kit, or the things that had happened because I *hadn't* forgiven myself—but I knew I had to try. I had to forgive myself. Something I should've done in the first place. I'd begun to forgive *her*, and if I could do that?

I had denied that my mistakes, my sins, were a part of me—and gone through hell trying to make that lie true. There was no such thing as a clean state. What I did is done. What happened, happened.

The liar, the thief, and now the killer. They were pieces of me. Bricks.

Masonry. I chortled.

"What?" Kit asked.

"Just being a nerd," I said. Another piece of me.

"I'm ready," I said. She squeezed my hand again, and the heaviness dissolved. A ribbon of warmth replaced it.

The bailiff put my cuffs back on and escorted me to the defendant's table. Gail went to the podium and made official introductions with the judge and prosecutor for the arraignment. The judge, a graying Latino man, studied me for a moment, then put on glasses to read the charges. The main one being murder in the second degree of Erik Marshall. An inward laugh, bitter and cold, cut through me. I'd been innocent when they started a manhunt for a murderer, but in the end I'd proved them right.

I looked behind me at the gallery. There was a part of me that wished Kamilah was here. The part of me that imagined the disgust on her face had won out, and I hadn't contacted her. She was always part of *After This*, always the centerpiece of my vision for the future. The plan was that I'd reach out when I'd proven myself to be the "day-in, day-out, good man" she deserved. She'd stay this time. We'd walk the woods together, hand in hand, our big scruffy mutt bounding ahead. I'd kiss her hand, she'd smile and swing our arms. That plan was dead.

Ortiz hadn't shown. He hadn't responded to calls or texts either. What happened to his girls—because of me—had broken things between us. The brokenness left a gnawing pit in my core, and I put a wall around it, forcing myself to ignore it, forcing myself to focus on those who *had* shown. Kevin Luo, sitting in the back wearing a neck brace, gave me a stoic nod. He'd written up a long report—a confession, really—of his role in the Del Rio incident that was now circulating the FBI bureaucracy. The Good Doctor— Anna Del Rosario—sat in the back too, a sad frown on her face. She had also put in a statement. Now that Marshall was gone, it was safe. The Feds had also gained access to Marshall's encrypted messages with Curione—if that was even his real name. Hallenbeck sat in the first row, holding Rita's hand in his lap. Kit was in the seat next to them. There were good people here to support me.

A thief, a liar, a killer, a nerd. A friend. A son. A man who will do what he must to protect those he loves and damn what it costs.

Finished, the judge shuffled the papers away and asked me

to the podium. I drifted there with my heartbeat humming in my head. The judge regarded me over his glasses. I met his gaze even as my legs turned to jelly. I gripped the podium to stay upright.

"Do you understand these charges?"

"Yes, Your Honor." My breaths puffed shallow and fast.

"How do you plead?"

I let the tension go and it fell away in cooling waves. I steadied my breathing.

"Guilty, Your Honor."

Mason Jones will return.

JOIN THE CONVERSATION

Sign up for Anthony DeCapite's author newsletter and you'll get a free exclusive: the story of Mace and Caleb confronting their mother's meth dealer.

https://bit.ly/decapitenews

ACKNOWLEDGMENTS

First, a big thank you to Justin Vaughn, who provided much-needed accountability and support throughout the writing process. In addition, I owe a debt to the folks who were willing to share their firsthand experiences with incarceration and parole. Mike, Jaime Camargo, and Erica Thompson, thank you. These experiences provided the emotional foundation for Mason's starting point in the story.

A big thanks to my alpha readers Jack Bentele, David Cobbins, and Elise DeCapite, who provided insightful and invaluable feedback. This book is better because of you! Alesia Gainer, thanks for reading and thank you for your encouragement. Carly Hayward, my developmental editor, thank you for once again getting me to dive deeper into Mace's emotional journey. You also made this book so much better.

I've been on my own journey, as an author, and I appreciate Katie McCoach being generous with her time and advice regarding it. Tayler Henderson, thank you for helping me find some perspective on that journey, too.

I was very fortunate to get help from Dwight Leggett, MD, on the medical background for Hallenbeck's TBI and other traumatic injuries. He also provided some cool descriptions and precursors for descriptions used in those areas. Thank you to the folks at the Westside Hope Center for being so welcoming. What I experienced there helped me make Kit more dimensional.

Any mistakes (or creative liberties) regarding real-life issues such as medical trauma and parole are entirely on me.

I had a fine group of people to help me finalize this bad boy. My beta readers, Sabrina Chase and Noah. My copy editor and proofreader, Sean Leonard. Stewart Williams formatted the manuscript for print and digital. Thank you all! Your professionalism and attention to detail was invaluable.

I'm grateful to everyone who helped me bring Mason Jones's latest journey into the world.

ABOUT THE AUTHOR

Anthony DeCapite writes breathless thrillers brimming with grit, honesty, and intensity. He served in the Marine Corps as a Combat Videographer, deploying to cyclone-stricken Bangladesh and to the remote islands of the southern Philippines. The real-life humanitarian crises he experienced during his service continue to influence his work. Anthony lives in Los Angeles with his faithful dog Sammy.

anthonydecapite.com

Made in the USA
Las Vegas, NV
17 December 2024

14534779R00152